James Edmund Harting, A. I Shand

The Rabbit

With a chapter on cookery

James Edmund Harting, A. I Shand

The Rabbit
With a chapter on cookery

ISBN/EAN: 9783744795449

Printed in Europe, USA, Canada, Australia, Japan

Cover: Foto ©Andreas Hilbeck / pixelio.de

More available books at **www.hansebooks.com**

THE RABBIT

FUR, FEATHER, AND FIN SERIES.

EDITED BY A. E. T. WATSON.

⁎ *The Volumes are also issued half-bound in leather, with gilt
top. The price can be had from all Booksellers.*

THE PARTRIDGE. *NATURAL HISTORY*—By the
Rev. H. A. MACPHERSON.——*SHOOTING*—By A. J. STUART-
WORTLEY.——*COOKERY*—By GEORGE SAINTSBURY. With
11 Illustrations and various Diagrams. Crown 8vo. 5s.

THE GROUSE. *NATURAL HISTORY*—By the Rev.
H. A. MACPHERSON.——*SHOOTING*—By A. J. STUART-
WORTLEY.——*COOKERY*—By GEORGE SAINTSBURY. With
13 Illustrations and various Diagrams. Crown 8vo. 5s.

THE PHEASANT. *NATURAL HISTORY*—By the
Rev. H. A. MACPHERSON.——*SHOOTING*—By A. J. STUART-
WORTLEY.——*COOKERY*—By ALEXANDER INNES SHAND.
With 10 Illustrations and various Diagrams. Crown 8vo. 5s.

THE HARE. *NATURAL HISTORY*—By the Rev.
H. A. MACPHERSON.——*SHOOTING*—By the Hon. GERALD
LASCELLES.——*COURSING*—By CHARLES RICHARDSON.——
HUNTING—By J. S. GIBBONS and G. H. LONGMAN.
——*COOKERY*—By Col. KENNEY HERBERT. With 9 Illus-
trations. Crown 8vo. 5s.

RED DEER. *NATURAL HISTORY.*—By the Rev.
H. A. MACPHERSON.——*DEER-STALKING*—By CAMERON
OF LOCHIEL.——*STAG-HUNTING*—By Viscount EBRING-
TON.——*COOKERY*—By ALEXANDER INNES SHAND. With
10 Illustrations. Crown 8vo. 5s.

THE SALMON. By the Hon. A. E. GATHORNE-HARDY.
With Chapters on the *LAW OF SALMON-FISHING*
by CLAUD DOUGLAS PENNANT; and *COOKERY* by ALEX-
ANDER INNES SHAND. With 8 Illustrations. Crown 8vo. 5s.

THE TROUT. By the MARQUESS OF GRANBY. With
Chapters on *BREEDING* by Col. F. H. CUSTANCE; and
COOKERY by ALEXANDER INNES SHAND. With 12 Illustra-
tions. Crown 8vo. 5s.

THE RABBIT. By JAMES EDMUND HARTING. With
a Chapter on *COOKERY* by ALEXANDER INNES SHAND.
With 10 Illustrations. Crown 8vo. 5s.

WILDFOWL. By the Hon. JOHN SCOTT-MONTAGU,
&c. With Illustrations. [*In preparation.*

LONGMANS, GREEN & CO., 39 Paternoster Row, London
New York and Bombay.

'HERE'S ONE SITTING'

THE RABBIT

BY

JAMES EDMUND HARTING

WITH A CHAPTER ON
COOKERY
BY ALEXANDER INNES SHAND

ILLUSTRATIONS BY ARCHIBALD THORBURN, G. E. LODGE
S. ALKEN AND CHARLES WHYMPER

LONGMANS, GREEN, AND CO.
39 PATERNOSTER ROW, LONDON
NEW YORK AND BOMBAY
1898

PREFACE

THE design of the *Fur, Feather, and Fin Series* is to present monographs, as complete as they can possibly be made, on the various English birds, beasts and fishes which are generally included under the head of Game.

Books on Natural History cover such a vast number of subjects that their writers necessarily find it impossible to deal with each in a really comprehensive manner ; and it is not within the scope of such works exhaustively to discuss the animals described, in the light of objects of sport. Books on sport, again, seldom treat at length of the Natural History of the creatures which are shot or otherwise taken ; and, so far as the Editor is aware, in no book hitherto published on Natural History or Sport has information been given as to the best methods of turning the contents of the bag to account.

Each volume of the present Series will, therefore, be devoted to a bird, beast, or fish. Their origin will be traced, their birth and breeding described, every known method of circumventing and killing them—not omitting the methods employed by the poacher—will be explained with special regard to modern developments, and they will only be left when on the table in the most appetising forms which the delicate science of cookery has discovered.

ALFRED E. T. WATSON.

CONTENTS

ILLUSTRATIONS

BY

A. Thorburn, G. E. Lodge, S. Alken and C. Whymper.

(Reproduced by the Swan Electric Engraving Company)

THE RABBIT

CHAPTER I

NATURAL HISTORY OF THE RABBIT

As a 'beast of warren' the rabbit has been well known in England for many centuries. Whether it is indigenous to this country, or whether, like the pheasant, the swan, and the fallow deer, it was introduced by the Romans, as some have asserted, is a question which, for want of direct evidence, will perhaps never be satisfactorily settled. We have it on the authority of the Yorkshire antiquary Whitaker that we are indebted to Roman enterprise, not only for the introduction of the rabbit, but also for the ferret, which they employed to hunt it; and the Latin names for these animals, *cuniculus* and *furectus*, both of which are described by Pliny,[1] give some colour to the assertion.

From what is stated by Greek and Latin authors,

---

[1] *Hist. Nat.* viii. 55.

it may be safely inferred that in early times the rabbit was not indigenous either in Greece or Italy, nor was it known eastward of these countries. The ancient Jews were unacquainted with it, and there is no mention of it in the Bible ; for it is now generally acknowledged that the Hebrew word *sháphan*, which, in the Authorised Version, is rendered 'coney of the rock,' is not our familiar rodent, but the Syrian Hyrax (*Hyrax syriacus*). The ancient classic authors, then, derived their knowledge of it through the early explorers of Western Europe. Strabo, writing about the year 50 B.C., expressly mentions the rabbit as being abundant in Spain. He writes: 'Of destructive animals there are scarcely any with the exception of certain little hares which burrow in the ground (πλὴν τῶν γεωρύχων λαγιδέων) and destroy both seeds and plants by gnawing at the roots. They are met with throughout almost the whole of Spain, extending to Marseilles, and infesting the islands also. It is said that formerly the inhabitants of the islands Majorca and Minorca sent a deputation to the Romans soliciting that a new land might be given them, as they were quite driven out of their country by those animals, being no longer able to stand against their vast multitudes.' Further on he observes that to check the increase of these 'little hares,' many ways of hunting have been devised, amongst others by wild weasels from Africa trained for the purpose (Καὶ δὴ γαλᾶς ἀγρίας ἃς ἡ Λιβύη φέρει τρέφουσιν ἐπίτηδες). Having muzzled these, they turn them into the holes, where they either drag out the animals they find there with their claws, or compel them to fly to the surface, where they are taken by people standing by for that purpose.[1]

Ælian, also, who lived in the third century of the Christian era, particularly describes the rabbits of Spain.[2] Pliny says : ' There is also a species of hare in Spain, which is called *cuniculus* ; it is extremely prolific, and produces famine in the Balearic islands, by destroying the harvests.' Further on he adds : ' It is a well-known fact that the inhabitants of the Balearic islands begged of the late Emperor Augustus the aid of a number of soldiers to prevent the too rapid increase of these animals. Ferrets (*viverræ*) are much prized on account of their hunting these animals ; they are put into the burrows, with their numerous outlets, which the rabbits form, and from which circumstance they derive their name ; and as the ferrets drive them out, they are taken above. '[3] The Latin word *cuniculus* denotes both a rabbit and an underground passage.

---

[1] *Geograph.* iii. 2, §6.   [2] *Hist. Nat.* xiii. 15.
[3] *Hist. Nat.* viii. 55.

Varro[1] suggests that the rabbit derived its name from the burrow it forms, and Martial avers that rabbits first taught men to undermine enemies' towns.[2]

Cognate with the Latin *cuniculus* we have the Italian *coniglio*, Spanish *conejo*, Belgic *konin*, Danish and Swedish *kaning*, German *kaninchen*, Old French *connin*, Welsh *cwningen*, and Old English *conyng* and *coney*, which, indeed, is our oldest name for the animal. The word rabbit, anciently *rabbet*, was originally applied only to the young animal. In the *Promptorium Parvulorum* (1440) we find 'Rabet, a yonge conye,' apparently derived through a French source, as indicated by the diminutive termination, *ette*. In Russell's 'Book of Nurture' (1424) we find *rabbettes*. At the present day, as everyone knows, the name rabbit is bestowed indifferently on young and old.

Another name for the animal, to be found in ancient books on hunting, is *riote*, the use of which may be here referred to incidentally as explaining the meaning of the phrase 'to run riot.' In an old MS. preserved in the Bodleian Library we may read the following instructive directions to a huntsman :—

'What rache (*i.e.* a hound hunting by scent) that renneth to a conyng yn any tyme, hym aughte to be ascryed (*i.e.* assailed with a shout), saying to hym

---

[1] *De Re Rustica*, iii. 12, §6. [2] *Epigr.* xiii. 60.

loude *war ryote war !* for noon other wylde beest yn
Ingelande is called *ryote* saf the conyng alonly.'

The structural differences between a rabbit and a
hare are chiefly apparent in the skull, and the relative
length of the ears and hind limbs, which are much
shorter in the rabbit than in the hare. In the latter
animal we note the greater complexity of the maxillo-
turbinal bones, and Professor Rolleston, commenting
upon this, observed, 'It is obvious that the rabbit,
living usually in a subterranean atmosphere, is
advantaged by having that atmosphere warmed as
much as possible before entering the lungs.'

The dentition in both hare and rabbit is typical
of a rodent or gnawing animal. Four large incisors,
two in the upper and two in the lower jaw, are formed
of hard bone (dentine), the front surfaces being composed of layers of very hard enamel. In the natural
condition these teeth are in opposition, and wear
each other away in the act of gnawing. The hard
enamel in the upper pair cuts away the softer dentine
in the lower, leaving the sharp front edge of enamel
standing up like the edge of a chisel, and the lower
perform the same duty for the upper. Thus four
sharp chisel-edged teeth are formed, which act most
efficiently in gnawing the hard food of the rodent,
such as bark or roots. If by any accident the lower

jaw of the animal is displaced, as occasionally happens from the impact of a shot, the incisors in the fractured jaw are distorted, and do not meet those above them, and as they are not then worn away by use, they continue to grow, sometimes to an extraordinary length. The manner in which animals thus deformed adapt themselves to new conditions is marvellous. They not only contrive to feed, but to live a long time after the injury, as shown by the ossified condition of the fracture when at length it comes to be examined. The different mode in which hares and rabbits feed is noteworthy. A Suffolk farmer, who is a good sportsman as well as shrewd observer of facts connected with natural history, asserts that you may generally tell whether your turnips are nibbled by hares or rabbits by the difference in the mode of attacking the roots. A hare will bite off the peel and leave it on the ground ; a rabbit will eat peel and all. There is a marked difference also in the method pursued by a rabbit and a rat when eating a turnip, as observed by Mr. R. M. Barrington. If the turnip is growing, and a portion of the bulb is still in the ground, a rat generally eats all round it and leaves the centre for the last ; whereas a rabbit begins at one side and works right through to the other side. A rat will bite off the rind, as a hare does, and will leave it in chips on the ground; a rabbit, as just remarked, will eat peel and all. Rats very often will leave a turnip half eaten to go to another; but if they mean to consume the bulb, they invariably finish in the middle. The top falls over at last with a truncated portion of the bulb attacked.

In pointing out some of the most marked differences which exist between a rabbit and a hare, allusion has been made *inter alia* to that which exists in the relative length of the limbs, and this is correlated with the different mode of retreat adopted by the two species. A rabbit seeks safety by concealment in a burrow; a hare seeks safety in flight. Obviously the greater length of the hind legs in the latter animal gives greater power and speed, and this is especially noticeable when a hare is going uphill. The shorter limbs of the rabbit are useful in other ways, namely, for throwing out the soil behind it when burrowing, and for giving the alarm to its companions by thumping on the ground, and so attracting the attention of those within hearing.

The advantage of having a white under-surface to the tail is also apparent on reflection; for when, on the approach of an intruder while rabbits are out feeding, those nearest to him begin to scuttle away, the little white flag in motion at once attracts the attention of others, and all speedily make for their burrows.

One of the most important differences between the rabbit and hare is the condition of the young at birth. In the case of the former, the young are born underground, and are blind at birth;[1] in the case of the latter they are deposited in a 'form' on the surface of the ground, and are born with the eyes open. This difference is correlated, no doubt, with the divergent habits of the two species ; for the very young leverets are so soon able to move away from the place of their birth that they do not stand in need of the same protection and concealment as the blind and helpless young of the coney.

The wild rabbit will begin to breed at the age of six months, and may have half a dozen litters in a year. Early rabbits will breed the same year. The period of gestation is twenty-eight days, and the number of young in a litter is generally from five to seven.

[1] In the case of a rabbit in captivity it was observed that the doe went 29 days with young, which were not only born blind but with their ears closed ; nor could they move them until the tenth day. On the eleventh day they began to see ; on the twelfth their ears were quite open, and on the thirteenth day they could erect their ears. They shed their first coat when about three months old.

Instances in which rabbits have produced their young aboveground, like hares, have been occasionally reported, but cannot be regarded as common. A good deal depends upon the nature of the soil in the locality frequented by them. For example, on moors where the soil is very wet, rabbits will sometimes refrain from burrowing, and content themselves with runs and galleries formed in the long matted heather and herbage. In very stony ground, too, where burrowing is more laborious, they will sometimes merely scratch a slight hollow, and make a 'form' like a hare. In *The Field* of December 2, 1876, Mr. W. Southam, of Durrington, near Amesbury, reported a typical case of a rabbit breeding above ground. On November 27, a flat 'form,' like that of a hare, was found in turnips, and contained four newly born young. Unluckily the old doe was shot as she left the 'form' before it was discovered. Another observer, Mr. John Cordeaux, of Great Cotes, Lincolnshire, found four young rabbits a few days old in a bare fallow field in the Humber marshes. They were nestling together in a slight hollow bedded with down. There was no covert or shelter whatever for them, the nest being as bare and exposed as that of a lapwing. In some cases in which newly born young have been found aboveground, it is quite likely that they may have been temporarily removed by the parent from some source of danger, as, for example, the flooding of the burrow by heavy rain. Under such circumstances these animals will quickly remove their young, carrying them one at a time in the mouth, as a cat does her kittens. One of the oddest places in which to find young rabbits, that we can call to mind, was the body of a 'scarecrow.' It had lain in a field, near Oakham, since the previous autumn, and consisted of an old bag stuffed with straw. Inside this, the following spring, were found five young rabbits.[1]

Although the regular breeding season with rabbits is from February until September, does in young are sometimes killed as late as November[2]; but this is not a common occurrence, and is perhaps to be attributed to the prevalence at the time of very mild and open weather.

The practice of ferreting and shooting rabbits after the close of the shooting season, say, after the

---

[1] Although many cases have been reported of hares going to ground, generally when pursued and hard pressed, we are not aware that any instance has been noted of a hare producing young in a burrow. White hares constantly seek refuge in rocks—that is, in holes under rocks and stones.

[2] *The Field*, December 14, 1889.

first of February, has always seemed to us a repre-
hensible one. As above stated, rabbits begin to
breed in February, and while there can be no satisfaction in shooting does that are scarcely able to run,
a great deal of cruelty is thoughtlessly perpetrated by
killing rabbits whose young ones are consequently
left to die of starvation in the burrow. Keepers, by
way of excuse, will assert that they have not had time
to kill the rabbits by the end of the shooting season.
But this is nonsense. There is plenty of time if they
choose to do it, and without disturbing the coverts
too, for they can ferret and catch them in nets, a
proceeding which, if quietly and properly carried
out, will not unduly disturb the pheasants. In our
opinion, rabbits should not be maintained in such
numbers that they cannot be killed down, so far as
is necessary, between September 1 and February 1.
Humanitarians, no doubt, would advocate a close
time for rabbits in the spring; but, in view of the
extraordinary rate at which these animals increase,
and the adverse nature of existing legislation, as indicated by the Ground Game Act of 1880, it is extremely
doubtful whether such a measure would be generally
acceptable.

One may tell an old rabbit from a young one
by feeling the joints of the forelegs. When the

extremities of the two bones which unite to form the joint are so close together that no space can be felt between them, the rabbit is an old one. On the other hand, if there is a perceptible separation at the joint the animal is a young one, and is more or less so as the bones are more or less separated. Another mode of distinguishing the two is by the claws, which in an old rabbit are very long and rough, in a young one short and smooth. The latter also has a softer coat.

When fresh killed a rabbit will be stiff and the flesh white and dry; when stale it will be limp, and the flesh will have a bluish tinge.

When taken young and domesticated, wild rabbits not only become soon accustomed to the altered conditions of life, but will live for many years in captivity. One, which was captured in Buckinghamshire when about ten days old and brought to London, had the run of the house and area, was tame, amusing, and cleanly in its habits. It would follow the cook about like a dog, and was a constant playmate in the nursery. In these circumstances it lived for six years.[1]

A wild rabbit, which had been captured in February, 1873, when only a few weeks old, and was

[1] *The Field*, July 16, 1892.

brought up by hand, was reported to be alive and well in its eleventh year.[1]

The average weight of a wild rabbit may be set down at from 3 lb. to 3½ lb., or about the same weight as a good wild mallard, or a cock pheasant ; but, as in the case of pheasants, much depends upon the abundance or otherwise of food, and the difference in weight between rabbits on a light soil, with nothing but innutritious grass to feed upon, and those from highly cultivated farm-lands, growing plenty of roots and clover, is very noticeable. In *The Field* of December 3, 1892, it was noted that a rabbit, shot in Lincolnshire, weighed 4 lb. 10 oz., and several have been recorded which weighed considerably over 4 lb.[2] An old buck, killed in the snow just before Christmas, weighed 4 lb. 13 oz. before being paunched, and this was in a district where no fresh stock had been introduced to increase the size. Under similar conditions, at Newport Pagnell, in January, 1890, one which attracted attention from its size was found to turn the scales at 4 lb. 14 oz.

Rabbits weighing 5 lb. and upwards, although of course not common, have several times been reported. One such, killed at Hambleton, South Buckingham-

---

[1] *The Zoologist*, 1883, p. 173.

[2] See *The Field* of September 30, 1893 ; October 17 and November 21, 1896.

shire, weighed 5 lb. 2 oz. ; and another, caught by a
dog at East Molesey, just below Tagg's Island, was
stated to have weighed 5 lb. 10 oz. *when paunched.*[1]
Λ correspondent at Lichfield wrote word, in February,
1890, that he had obtained one which weighed 6 lb.
all but 2 oz., and was of opinion that it was a pure-
bred wild rabbit.

When so-called wild rabbits of such extraordinary
size are reported, there is naturally some reason to
suspect that they must be the result of a cross with
tame rabbits, that have been turned down, if not on
the same ground, at all events on adjoining land ;
and in some cases this has been proved to be so.
For example, in *The Field* of February 14, 1891,
Mr. G. M. Chamberlain, of Stratton Strawless, near
Norwich, wrote to report that he had shot a rabbit in
one of the coverts there, which weighed no less than
6½ lb. ; but the following week a former agent on
the estate announced that he well remembered several
half-bred animals being killed there in 1881, and that
on inquiry he had discovered that tame ones had
been turned down to increase the size, and that
some killed that year were marked with white.

We regard it as a mistake to turn down tame
rabbits on a sporting estate, for although the result no

[1] *The Field,* January 7, 1888.

doubt will be to increase the size of the progeny, that is not what is wanted if they are to afford sport with the gun, and tame rabbits will not burrow, but live on the surface like hares. The *desideratum* is a strong active rabbit with the highest possible turn of speed, and not a clumsy animal that can hardly be made to move. In a warren, of course, where rabbits are only reared for market, and are always ferreted and netted, or trapped, the case is different; speed counts for nothing, and the heavier the animal the better will be the market price obtained.

Size may be increased by cutting if desired,[1] although for sporting purposes, as above remarked, no advantage will be gained therefrom.

It is remarkable that insular forms are always much smaller than those on a mainland, and a notable instance of this may be observed in the rabbits on the island of Porto Santo, Madeira. This feral breed, however, is known to have descended from some which were turned down about the year 1418 by Gonzales Zarco. They are now much smaller than their European relatives, being nearly one-third less in weight; the upper parts are much redder and the lower surface greyer, while the tail is reddish brown above.

[1] Daniel, vol. i. p. 486.

Rabbits exist on the Saltee and Keragh Islands off the coast of Wexford, and on the Island of Inishtrahull, Co. Donegal; but evidence is wanting to show whether they are smaller, lighter in weight, or darker in colour. This might be ascertained, and it would be interesting also to obtain statistics on these points from some of the western isles of Scotland ; for instance, from the Isle of Handa, Sutherlandshire, where rabbits are very abundant.

Within certain limits, wild rabbits are subject to some variation in colour, without any admixture from tame stock. White, black, sandy, and silver-grey are all well-known varieties, and although they cannot be said to be common, several localities might be mentioned in which there is an unusual preponderance of either white or black ones.[1] White ones may be seen any day in Bosworth Park, Leicester, and on the estate of Mr. Joseph Lescher, of Boyles Court, Essex ; and black ones occur sporadically in Cheshire, notably in the large warrens of Lyme Park, and not infrequently in the coverts of Mr. Assheton Smith, of Vaynol, North Wales. Dr. Laver, in his recently published work on the mammalian fauna of Essex,

---

[1] See *The Zoologist*, 1866, p. 385; and *The Essex Naturalist*, vol. ii. p. 33, and vol. iii. p. 25.

states that a silver-grey rabbit is generally black in its first coat.

'Silver-greys' can be readily reared in the open, and there is no difficulty in keeping them apart from the ordinary wild stock ; but they have nothing to recommend them from the sportsman's point of view, and the value of their skins at the present day is hardly sufficient to warrant any special outlay in rearing them.

The question whether rabbits and hares ever interbreed is one that is frequently asked, and apparently many persons believe in its possibility. They point to the so-called 'Belgian Hare' or 'Leporine,' which they assert is a well-known hybrid between these two species. That the animal is well known there is no doubt ; it appears at every rabbit and poultry show of importance, and special prizes are offered for the most typical specimens. Its appearance, too, is that of a hybrid hare ; but the resemblance is merely superficial. About forty years ago a breed of rabbits originated in Belgium which somewhat distantly resembled the ordinary brown hare, and some enterprising breeder pretended that he had succeeded in crossing the hare with a rabbit, and that these were the produce. Since this introduction the so-called 'Leporines' have been bred repeatedly, with

C

a twofold object—to increase size, and ostensibly to develop a rabbit of the form, colour, and fur of the wild hare.

After what has been stated above as to the very different condition of the rabbit and hare at birth— the young of the former being naked and blind, while those of the latter are clothed with fur and with their eyes open—it needs not much reflection to conclude that a cross between these two animals is a physio-logical impossibility. No scientific investigator who has taken due precautions has ever succeeded in obtaining such a hybrid.

The so-called 'Leporine' is merely a large domesticated variety of the common rabbit, resem-bling a hare in form and colour. On examination it will be found that its forelegs are not above half the length of those of the common hare, and if the fur of the back be turned up, it will be seen that the hair next the skin is quite dark instead of light coloured. The experiment of turning out 'Belgian Hares' for the purpose of increasing the size of the ordinary wild rabbit has often been made, and with partial success ; but as they are very tame and confiding, and never go to ground (for tame rabbits never burrow), they easily fall a prey to vermin and poachers. If it is desired to increase the size of the rabbits on ground where they are reared only for the market, and not for sporting purposes, the best mode of procedure is to net a wild buck rabbit and place it with a Belgian doe in a partially darkened loose box in a stable otherwise unused. When they have been long enough together, the buck should be restored to liberty, and the offspring, when weaned, turned into different burrows. It will not answer so well to catch a wild doe and place it with a Belgian buck, for the wild doe does not breed so readily in captivity. The progeny in the former case always resemble the wild rabbit more than the so-called Belgian hare.

The rabbit is usually regarded as one of the most timid of animals, seldom permitting a very near approach (unless when in a 'seat' it believes itself to be undiscovered) and usually taking to flight at the least alarm. The case is different, however, when a doe has young to look after. Her maternal courage is then displayed in a way that is sometimes astonishing.

One day in September 1890, while Mr. Randolph, of Modbury, Wiltshire, was passing through a wood, he observed a weasel hunting a young rabbit about the size of a man's fist. He stood still to watch the result. The chase did not last long, for the young rabbit soon gave up, and the weasel killed it. An old rabbit, presumably the parent, suddenly dashed out upon the scene from a bank, and fairly 'went for' the weasel. The latter turned tail at once and abandoned his prey. But the old rabbit still continued to follow him with the greatest fury till she had driven him completely off the ground.

On another occasion, in October, 1891, a gamekeeper in the service of Mr. Deacon, of Southborough, Tunbridge Wells, on going through a wood saw a stoat which had caught a young rabbit, playing with it as a cat does with a mouse, letting it go and then catching it again. Before the keeper could interfere, he saw a full-grown rabbit, probably the doe, rush out of some underwood close by, knock over the stoat, and carry off the young one in its mouth. The stoat, on recovering itself, followed through the underwood, but presently reappeared in retreat pursued by a couple of rabbits.

A friend of the writer resident in North Wales was once witness to a similar incident when the aggressor was a crow. A young rabbit had strayed a little too far from the mouth of the burrow, when a carrion crow suddenly alighted close to it, and in a series of hops gave chase, and was about to seize it. Suddenly from the mouth of the burrow an old rabbit came with a rush, and going full tilt at the crow,

MATERNAL INSTINCT

knocked it over before it could get out of the way. The discomfited bird, with a hoarse croak, scrambled on to its feet and hastily took flight.

Nor are these exceptional cases. Similar instances of the courageous behaviour of rabbits in defence of their young have been from time to time recorded.[1]

In one of the instances above related it will be observed that the parent rabbit, after driving away a stoat, carried off her young one in her mouth. It is, perhaps, not generally known that both hares and rabbits transport their young in this way, just as cats will carry their kittens, or dogs their puppies. Many such instances have come under our notice, more often in the case of hares, which convey their young in this manner, when they have been discovered, to a place of greater safety.

It is somewhat curious that, notwithstanding the fierce way in which both rabbits and hares will defend their young, they seldom attempt to bite anyone when taken from a net, or on being picked up when wounded by shot. The writer in twenty-five years' experience, during which time he must have shot and seen others shoot thousands of rabbits, has never

[1] See Couch, *Illustrations of Instinct*, p. 231 ; *The Essex Naturalist*, vol. ii. (1888), p. 71 ; *The Field*, September 8, 1888, September 20, 1890, November 7, 1891, May 7, 1892, October 7, 1893, and August 14, 1897.

personally witnessed anything of the kind. Presumably, therefore, such instances are rare, although, from time to time, a few have been recorded. The head-keeper at Craigincat, Perthshire, reported, in January, 1894, that, having shot at and wounded a rabbit, he sent a spaniel to retrieve it, when to his surprise he heard the dog howling. On running to see what was the matter, he found that the rabbit had caught hold of the dog by the lip, and the dog was howling and swinging the rabbit round and round trying to get rid of it. Eventually the rabbit let go, and the dog retrieved it. A somewhat similar case was reported by Mr. S. E. Moony, of The Doon, Athlone. His keeper was about to take a rabbit out of a trap, and had seized it by the hind legs, when the rabbit made a sudden snap at the man's other hand and fixed its teeth in his thumb sufficiently deep to draw blood. Although this man had been engaged in trapping rabbits for nearly thirty years, he stated that he never before knew a rabbit to retaliate.

In December, 1893, Mr. H. Selby, of Stoborough, near Wareham, was severely bitten by a rabbit that he was picking up after it had been shot through the hind quarters. Its teeth met through the thickest part of the flesh inside the third finger of the right hand, and the wound, having begun to fester, had to be poulticed. Mr. Eustace Banks, of the Rectory, Corfe Castle, who reported the case in *The Field* of February 17, 1894, mentioned this as the only instance of a wounded rabbit biting that had come to his knowledge, and he considered it therefore of very rare occurrence. On the other hand, Mr. J. Simpson, of Wortley, Yorkshire, whose excellent book on the rabbit we shall have occasion to quote later on, thus commented on the occurrence : ' Until reading the notes which have appeared lately in *The Field*, I was under the impression that it was pretty well known that rabbits would bite when provoked. I have been bitten a number of times by both tame and wild rabbits—the latter in a tame state —and on every occasion it happened when I had incautiously put my hand near a nest of young. The doe sprang with a bound at my hand and gave just one severe grip. I got so well aware of this when a boy, that I used always to collar the doe before putting my hand on the nest.'

Here, it will be observed, the attack was made *in defence of the young*, which is a different matter from the case of a rabbit biting when wounded, an event, as above stated, of fortunately rare occurrence.

As to the comparative speed of hares and rabbits

some difference of opinion prevails. On this point we are disposed to agree with Mr. Allan Gordon Cameron, of Ledaig, N.B., who, writing in *The Field* of November 30, 1895, gives the following result of his experience :—

' My brother and I used to course both hares and rabbits on Costa Hill in Orkney, where the turf is smooth and undulating, the grass, storm-swept with Atlantic spray, remarkably sweet, and the hares and rabbits constitutionally vigorous. A little greyhound bitch we had, who was wonderfully smart at getting away, used to account for most of the rabbits lying outside a radius of fifty yards, or thereabouts, from the burrow ; but she could not have picked up a hare in a similar distance ; and sometimes a strong hare dipping over the cliff after a long run, would fairly beat our four dogs—two of them powerful brutes, that would stop a deer single-handed. Our impression is that a rabbit gets up its top speed at once, and has no spurt at a pinch ; but a hare requires pressing, will not get properly extended unless pressed, and answers splendidly to every effort of the dogs that may be almost touching her.'

A rabbit is said to run faster than a hare for thirty-five yards ; and no one would think of comparing the two but for the few seconds that elapse after a rabbit is pushed from its 'seat'—when it runs its fastest—and after the hare is started, uncertain, timidly cantering off, but occasionally racing away at a speed which few four-footed creatures excel. The rabbit, with its short legs, only half the length of a hare's, and its shorter body, twists and swerves aside with a jerky motion, and really seems to be going at a tremendous pace. The hare, with her long legs, and the stride and grace of a racehorse, moves away so evenly that most people do not realise her true speed. No one who has shot at a hare can doubt her superior pace.

Sportsmen who shoot much over marshes, and districts where dykes and drains abound, must have noticed that hares, and occasionally rabbits also, will take to the water when hard pressed. Hares have a great liking for sitting out upon the higher ground of the saltings, and there, of course, when overtaken by a spring-tide, they are sometimes forced to swim the creeks in order to reach dry land. Rabbits probably have less occasion for exercising their swimming powers; nevertheless they have been occasionally observed to swim well. In October, 1897, Mr. H. Sharp, author of an excellent book on 'Wild Fowling,' was one of a party shooting hares on an Essex 'salting.' During the day much amusement was caused by the boldness of a rabbit, which, on being disturbed from a snug 'seat' in a tuft of grass, made straight for a wide creek, and entering the water, struck out boldly for the opposite side, carrying the head well elevated, and progressing at a good pace.

Mr. G. H. Warrender, of Springfields, Wolver-hampton, reported that one day in September, 1890, he was walking along a canal side, when he saw a young rabbit, apparently about a month old, on the towing-path. He chased it a few yards, when he was astonished to see it leap into the canal and swim like a water-rat to the far side. This occurred in the morning. He had occasion to pass the same spot in the evening, when he saw something plunge into the water on the towing-path side, which he thought at first sight was a water-rat, but on closer observa-tion, it proved to be a young rabbit—the same, probably, which he had seen leap into the canal in the morning. He pulled it out of the water and put it on dry land, when it ran off into a small covert, apparently little the worse for its aquatic adventure.

The appearance presented by a rabbit when swimming, as compared with a squirrel and stoat, is well shown in a sketch by Mr. J. G. Millais, at page 44 of his work on 'British Deer' (1897). For the purpose of obtaining accurate pictures of the various modes in which wild animals swim, he had live specimens caught and placed in the water, and then rowed alongside them for some distance, until he had made correct outline sketches.

Although rabbits are strictly speaking terrestrial rodents, they occasionally show a tendency to arboreal habits. Strange as it may appear, they will ascend the sloping trunks of trees, not only when pursued by a dog and no burrow is near, but also from choice. Naturally they climb best on a tree which has rough bark or ivy on it, and which has been blown or is leaning out of the perpendicular. Sometimes they will occupy the hollow of a decayed tree, at other times the crown of a pollard. Instances are on record of rabbits being found in such situations, at heights varying from seven to ten or twelve feet from the ground.[1] Colonel Hawker, in his 'Instructions to Young Sportsmen' (p. 256), mentions a case of a rabbit being found sitting in a tree; and a friend of the present writer claims to have accomplished the unique feat of shooting 'a rocketting rabbit,' which, on being dislodged from a tree, sprang into the air

[1] See *The Field* of December 20 and 27, 1879; January 10, 1880; July 7, 1888; March 14, 1896, and February 20 and 27, 1897.

and received a charge of No. 6 shot before it reached the ground !

Rabbits are unquestionably the kind of stock to make the finest turf ; they bite closer than any other animal that grazes, and the best turf for gardens is that taken from warrens, or from downs on which rabbits abound. Sandy commons, covered with furze, are a favourite resort of rabbits, and on such ground they often increase rapidly in numbers. The soil being light and friable is easily excavated, and the furze affords, not only a secure retreat, but a never-failing supply of food in the young tops of the plants, which are sufficiently tender before the spines have become matured.

In the choice of food rabbits do not appear to be very particular. They will eat almost anything that is green. Indeed, so destructive are they to most plants and young growing trees, that it is a matter of importance to game preservers, who want under-wood in the coverts as shelter for pheasants, to ascertain what shrubs are 'rabbit proof.' Common rhododendron, though not absolutely 'rabbit proof,' is not so liable to be attacked as many other shrubs. It will grow in shady places better than any other evergreen, especially if the soil is sandy and moist. But, although as a rule rabbits will not injure rhododendrons when the latter are well established, they will gnaw them when freshly planted, unless protected, like Aucubas. It is said that they will not touch *Rhododendron ponticum*, even if the plants are small and the winter severe. Nor will they feed upon Elder, which has the recommendation of growing well under trees, and when pleached (or 'plashed,' as it is termed locally) rabbits will lie well under it. They are not to be trusted near Hollies or young Osiers. Indeed they seem to be rather partial to Hollies, and in time of snow will attack even old trees. In hard weather, too, both Laurels and Privet suffer from their depredations. The larger kinds of Box, Snowberry plant (*Symphoricarpus*), and Butcher's Broom (*Ruscus aculeatus*) are recommended where the soil is favourable to their growth, and, for wet places, Scarlet Dogwood (*Cornus sanguinea*). In moist woods, too, a good thing to plant is *Carex pendula*, a common sedge, which forms good evergreen ground covert, and is very free. In like soil the Wood-rush, Briar, and Wood-grass (*Aira*) may be recommended.

In the way of berried shrubs nothing is more beautiful than a well-grown specimen of *Cotoneaster affinis*. Every year it is laden with bunches of glossy red berries. It is well adapted for planting along the edges of game coverts, as it affords plenty of food for pheasants, which are very fond of the berries. Probably the more it is exposed to the influence of the sun the more freely does it produce its beautiful clusters of fruit.

Apropos of ornamental plants, we may usefully give here, on the recommendation of Sir Herbert Maxwell, the following list, which he tells us [1] contains well-nigh all the ornamental shrubs which may be relied on to defy the attacks of rabbits; although there are others, such as the American Partridge berry (*Gaultheria*), and several kinds of Barberry which, if protected when first planted out, can take care of themselves afterwards :—

Azalea, rhododendron, honeysuckle, fly honeysuckle (*Lonicera xylosteum*), tree peony, lilac, syringa, snowberry, hardy fuchsia, spurge laurel (*Daphne laureola* and *Daphne mezereum*), St. John's wort, spindlewood (*Euonymus europæus*), guelder-rose (*Viburnum Opulus*), wayfaring-tree (*Viburnum Lantana*), laurustinus, cotoneaster, hawthorn, dogwood, sea buckthorn (*Hippophaë rhamnoides*), spiræa, deutzia, and all kinds of *Ribes* and arbutus.

Before leaving the subject of shrubs suitable for planting where rabbits and hares are numerous, it may not be superfluous to notice some that will thrive

[1] *Memories of the Months,* 1897, p. 92.

under the drip of trees ; for this is a matter of some importance in coverts composed of forest trees of large growth with very little underwood. Here it is not a question of food, but shelter, and nothing is more annoying to shooters when walking through such woods 'in line' than to see all the ground game going forward, just out of shot, for the reason that there is nothing to hide them. The owner of the covert will perhaps say he can get nothing to grow under the spread and drip of the trees. This need not necessarily be so. Several shrubs might be named which will thrive under such conditions; but the planter would be well advised if, instead of scattering the different kinds singly all over the ground at wide distances apart, he were to plant them in clumps— say, each plant three to four feet apart—and a mixture of a few kinds in masses, taking care to keep the low-growing and less straggling sorts next to the wood-rides. Amongst those adapted to such treatment may be mentioned : Common and Portugal laurels; *Rhododendron ponticum ; Azalea pontica ; Taxus baccata ; Ruscus aculeatus* and *R. hypoglossum ; Cotoneaster buxifolia, C. microphylla* and *C. Hookerii ; Pernettya mucronata* (for peat soils); *Phillyrea*, of sorts ; *Rhamnus alaternus ;* Broom ; *Leycesteria formosa ;* Box, of sorts ; *Juniperus communis* and *J. Sabina; Potentilla fruticosa; Buddleia globosa; Viburnum Lantana* and *V. Opulus; Gaultheria Shallon ; Ribes,* of sorts ; *Weigelia rosea ; Euonymus europæus; Berberis Aquifolium, B. dulcis, B. Darwinii, B. vulgaris,* and *B. vulgaris purpurea; Hippophaë rhamnoides,* and *H. angustifolia ; Arbutus Unedo ; Garrya elliptica ; Rosa rubiginosa ; Symphoria racemosa.*

A writer in the weekly journal *Woods and Forests* remarks : ' It is difficult to get two people to agree as to the trees with which rabbits and hares meddle. Some experienced planters say that these animals cut *Pinus Laricio* very much if planted small, but do not touch *Pinus austriaca.* Now, as for the latter, I can confidently assert that they cut it more than any other of the pine tribe. With me they have attacked and thoroughly destroyed fine plants of it four and five feet high. A neighbour, who has planted *Pinus Laricio* (I have none except guarded), says that it is ' rabbit proof,' and on his assertion I have now planted some hundreds. The fact is, I believe, in a really severe winter, rabbits will attack anything. In a deep snow I have had yews eaten down, but in the generality of years certain things escape.'

Yews cannot be recommended for planting in game coverts, for although the leaves may be eaten with impunity by rabbits, as is the case with goats, it is otherwise with pheasants, several instances having been reported in which these birds have been picked up dead, and found on examination to have their crops filled, or partly filled, with yew leaves.[1] Death seems to have been due to the action of the poisonous leaves producing inflammation of the digestive organs ; but why well-fed pheasants should sometimes eat yew leaves, and on other occasions pass them untouched, it is difficult to explain. Shirley mentions a case in which deer were poisoned by eating yew at Badminton in Gloucestershire.[2]

M. Barbier, of Orleans, writing in December, 1892, recommended the Corsican pine as the only tree untouched by rabbits where planted with *Pinus sylvestris* and black Austrian pine ; but this only shows that where several different kinds are growing together, the Corsican pine may be the least appreciated. In a woody district in Sussex, where a field was planted with this, it was found that nearly every plant was gnawed and injured. Although the shoots are not always eaten, they are often nibbled, and pieces taken off the bark, so as to cause the resinous sap to run down.

The unsightly appearance and cost of smearing make it of very little use. Extensive plantations are

[1] See *The Field*, November 25 and December 2, 1876 ; December 20, 1890 ; September 17, 1892, and November 11, 1893.
[2] *English Deer Parks*, p. 245.

often formed of small trees less than a foot high, and even if there were both time and means to smear the stems of every one of these little trees with one or other of the compounds which some people recommend, the rabbits would still take off the tops and leave the smeared stumps. The idea is absurd, from the standpoint of an extensive planter; for 20,000 trees, of the size referred to, do not go far in planting even a small field.

In young plantations where rabbits and hares abound there is nothing so effectual as wire-netting until the trees are strong enough and tall enough to be out of the way of their attacks.

For permanent protection the best fence is an iron-bar fence, wired with a one-inch mesh to the top, or, say, to a height of 4 ft., with 6 in. of wire underground; 3 ft. 6 in. might do as well, but generally it will be found best to wire to the top of an ordinary iron-bar fence, so that all danger from snow, leaves, and stock getting through may be effectually avoided. For larch plantations, and for temporary work, 3 ft. 6 in. wire may be used. As a rule, it is advisable to use simple iron supports for the wiring of young plantations, rather than stakes cut out of underwood for supporting the netting, as these rot very soon. Larch poles are an exception, however, and good stakes of larch, well put in, will probably last as long as the young wood needs protection.

Fences, designed to keep rabbits only out of young plantations, may be made to cost considerably less than one shilling per yard. A rabbit-warren fence 4 ft. high, with flap-turned top and bottom, is made of 1½ in. wire netting, 'strong,' 36 in. wide for the top of the fence, and 1¼ in. netting, 24 in. wide, for the bottom, costing together about 40s. per 100 yards ; stout oak stakes to match, one yard asunder, No. 4 galvanised wire rope for the top, double or single, annealed wire to support the turned-in flap, staples and labour, complete, all done by the piece, cost from 1s. to 1s. 3d. per yard run, and will resist cattle and horses.

It is, perhaps, not generally known that, in addition to old roots and hay, which make the best winter food, rabbits are fond of acorns, and fatten well on them. The oak, indeed, is an invaluable tree in game coverts ; for not only rabbits, but pheasants, wood-pigeons, and wild-ducks are all very partial to acorns, and feed greedily on them. Mr. J. Simpson, of Wortley, recommends them especially for feeding rabbits in warrens. Writing in *The Field* of December 9, 1893, he says :—

'For the last five years the rabbits in the warren

here have considerably exceeded the average weight
of wild rabbits, although I believe, and am told by
visitors, that the number on the ground is altogether
unprecedented; but this season (December, 1893)
they are larger and fatter than usual, which I attribute
to the unusually heavy crop of acorns shed by a
number of old oak trees growing here and there in
the warren. As soon as the acorns began to drop, the
rabbits attacked them, and now nothing but the husks
are left, scattered like chaff on the pasture, for the
rabbits eat the kernel only. I had the curiosity to
make a post-mortem examination of two killed pro-
miscuously for use, weighing together nearly 7 lb.
after paunching, and was struck by the large amount
of fat in both, the kidneys being quite bedded in fat.
Rabbits, such as you buy, are usually almost destitute
of fat, and in our case, no doubt, it is due to the rich
nourishing acorn food, which contains an enormous
percentage of potash, lime, and phosphoric acid. The
rabbits have been remarkably lively also, and the fur
of those killed is fine and dense. As acorns, when
moderately plentiful, can be collected by children for
8*d.* or 1*s.* per bushel, it will be understood what an
excellent and cheap supply of food is often available
for rabbit warrens, where a bushel goes a long way.
Acorns are often collected in this way for deer in

hundreds of bushels. As there has been no mortality among the rabbits worth mentioning, I conclude that acorns may be supplied freely in large quantities.'

In addition to acorns, such pasture as they can get for themselves may be supplemented by hay, crushed oats, and wood-cuttings for the sake of the bark. This of course applies rather to warrens and to places where the food is restricted by reason of enclosure with wire-netting.

Where rabbits are not restrained within certain limits, but are able to get out and roam where they list in quest of food, they can generally manage to get a living without any such assistance as that above indicated, even in districts which look most bare and . unproductive. It would not be supposed that there is much nourishment to be derived from sand-grass, for example; and yet, in the sand-hills by the sea the rabbits are generally in very good condition. The mention of sand-hills reminds us of a 'dodge' for bolting a rabbit without the aid of a ferret when the burrow happens to be within reach of the sea-shore, and the footprints of the occupant show that he is 'at home.' Having obtained a lively specimen of a shore crab, produce a piece of wax or composite candle, about an inch in length, and having stuck it on the back of the crab with a few drops of melted wax, light the wick, and start the bearer of it down the burrow. The rabbit will probably come out in such a hurry that the crab will be knocked over, and the light will be put out, but that will be of little consequence if the rabbit is also knocked over by a well-directed charge of shot.

If it were not for the extraordinary fecundity of the rabbit, the number of litters to which a doe will give birth in a year, and the number of young produced in each litter, the species *Lepus cuniculus*, with such a host of enemies, foremost of which is man, must long ago have become extinct. As if it were not enough to face the gun, and run the risk of capture by ferret, gin, brass wire, or drop-down net, the unfortunate 'Bunter' has a host of natural enemies to contend with, both furred and feathered. Foremost amongst these, perhaps, because so pertinacious a pursuer, hunting by scent, is the stoat (*Mustela erminea*), who need never go without a dinner where rabbits abound. He will not only enter a burrow like a ferret and cause the inmates to bolt, but will pursue a rabbit in the open like a foxhound, and sooner or later overtake and kill him. The present writer has on several occasions been an eye-witness of both these manœuvres, and, standing motionless to watch the performance, has been struck with the courage

STOAT HUNTING RABBIT

and pertinacity displayed by a stoat in attacking and vanquishing an animal so very much larger and heavier than itself. It has been already shown, however (p. 20), that in defence of her young a plucky doe rabbit finds courage enough to attack a stoat, and will even succeed in repulsing him altogether.

While the stoat will boldly hunt a rabbit *underground* (an example which its smaller relative the weasel essays to imitate, though, from its diminutive size, it can take toll of comparatively small rabbits, preferring mice and small birds), the fox will lie in wait for rabbits of any size when *aboveground*, and usually captures them by stealth or stratagem.

The badger will dig down upon the young at the end of a burrow and scratch them out, as may be seen by the marks of his claws in the soil, and bits of fluff that lie scattered about near the scene of his operations. There is, perhaps, no greater enemy to young rabbits than the common brown rat, not only on account of his ferocity, size, and weight, which amounts sometimes to 2 lb. and upwards,[1] but also because he comes not singly but in droves. During the summer months rats quit the barns, stables, out-houses and styes, where they have been hiding

[1] See *The Field* of January 11 and 18, 1896 ; January 2 and 9, 1897.

throughout the winter, and pilfering in all directions, and take to the woods and fields, just as Londoners quit town for change of air when the fine weather sets in. In the woods they take heavy toll of the pheasants' food, eggs, and young pheasants, too, when they are hatched, unless the gamekeeper looks sharp after them and keeps down their number. In the fields they take to the hedgerows, and especially frequent such banks as have been already perforated by rabbits. Here they have a fine time of it until the ratcatcher comes along with his ferrets and ' varmint ' dogs, and does his best to clear them out.

In a dry summer we are accustomed to hear complaints of a scarcity of rabbits, and the complainants usually attribute it to the drought. Probably the dry weather has nothing to do with it, and the true cause should be looked for in one of two directions : either the rats are out for their 'autumn manœuvres,' and the country wants ferreting, or the rabbits have been too long isolated, and fresh stock needs to be imported. They inter-breed to such an extent that if new blood be not introduced from time to time their numbers will eventually decrease.

From the above remarks it will be gathered that the stoat and the rat are rivals in the chase of the wild rabbit ; they are also deadly enemies. The stoat, like a good sportsman who hunts his quarry by scent, evidently looks upon the rat as a poacher, and whenever he encounters him in his hunting forays ' goes for him ' at once.

We have watched stoats hunting both rats and rabbits, and were once witness to a most determined fight, on a road which crosses a Sussex common, between an average-sized stoat and an enormous rat, which was certainly much heavier than its adversary. This fight, which was a trial of ' weight *versus* science,' ended in favour of the stoat, which killed its adversary and dragged it off the road into the furze on the common.

We are not at all in favour of exterminating stoats. Where rabbits are plentiful a few stoats will not do them much harm, and, as above hinted, will do good in keeping down the rats, and thus saving the pheasants' food and the pheasant chicks. Rats, being so much more numerous than stoats, will do much more mischief than the latter where game and rabbits are concerned.

The list of natural enemies of the rabbit would not be complete without mention of the cat, which, from its stealthy actions and skill in stalking, proves itself on occasions to be an expert rabbit-catcher. This is especially the case with the cats of cottagers who live

in proximity to game coverts. These animals get into
he habit of leading a roving life, gradually become
confirmed poachers, and sooner or later fall victims
to a trap or a charge of shot. Occasionally a cat
will take up its abode temporarily in a rabbit burrow,
and many instances are on record of cats being
bolted by ferrets, to the astonishment of those who
were anxiously expecting the appearance of a rabbit.[1]

The following note from Mr. R. B. Lee is to the
point. He writes : 'On two occasions, during a
period extending over about a dozen years, have I
been ferreting rabbits when a cat has bolted from the
hole. The first time I thought it a most unusual
occurrence ; the second time I was accompanied by a
gamekeeper and a clever rabbit-catcher, both of
whom had had previously a similar experience, and
said that a cat was more easily driven by a ferret than
any other animal. It is, however, but seldom a cat
lays up in a *bona fide* rabbit burrow. Some years
ago I shot over ground which included a large extent
of rock, in which there were crevices and long underground passages—not rabbit burrows properly, but
still holding a great number of rabbits. These holes
were favourite retreats for the semi-wild cats with which
the place was infested ; and certainly our ferrets had

[1] See *The Field*, February 14, 21, and 28, 1885.

often less difficulty in making them bolt than they
had the rabbits.'

It is, of course, well known that cats, when deprived
wholly or in part of their young, will suckle the young
of other animals, and they seem to take very kindly
to young rabbits. This usually happens when the
latter are purposely supplied to them ; but instances
are on record in which cats have been known to bring
home young rabbits on their own account, and nurse
them with care. Mr. H. D. Nadin, of Burton-on-
Trent, writing on May 17, 1890, says : 'A cat kept
by the blacksmiths in their shop at a colliery in which
I am interested, gave birth to three kittens a short
time ago. One of these died at once, and the mother
was much distressed by the loss. She accordingly
made a journey across some fields to a rabbit warren
distant about a hundred yards, whence she obtained
and carried back a young rabbit (about ten days old),
which she suckled along with the two remaining
kittens, treating it in every way as if it were her own
progeny. This she continued to do for four days, but
during that time she gradually became uneasy, as the
workmen persisted in coming to view the novel sight.
She then commenced to carry both the kittens and
rabbit about, and on the fifth day they were not
to be found. After a good search, however, the two

kittens were found alive under a heap of scrap iron, but the rabbit was not found until some time later, in a different part of the building ; but, when discovered, was unfortunately dead. The men left the rabbit with the cat, I suppose to convince her of its decease ; but, sad to relate, on returning a short time later, found she had made a meal of it. I regret the cat had not been removed to a quiet spot : but the fact that she herself carried a former lot of kittens to the place where these were born, led the men to suppose she would rest quietly where she was.'

So much for the 'furred enemies' of rabbits. Amongst their 'feathered foes' may be named the golden and white-tailed eagles, both of which prey on them habitually (as they do also upon hares), sweeping round a hillside, and carrying them off unawares before they can get to ground. Only last autumn a friend of the writer witnessed the capture of a rabbit by a golden eagle in Scotland, and as the great bird sailed away with its booty, which was held by the head in one foot, the body of the rabbit was seen swinging like a pendulum, as long as its captor remained in sight. The common buzzard, as well as the rough-legged buzzard, are both partial to rabbits, but take them in a different manner. They will sit on the limb of a tree at the edge of a covert, and wait till the rabbits come out to feed.   As soon as one of them gets far enough out from the fence, the buzzard will glide noiselessly down and pounce upon his back in an instant.   Escape is then hopeless, for the powerful talons grip him like a steel trap, and his fate is sealed. The goshawk is so good a rabbit-catcher that its skill in this respect is turned to excellent account by falconers, who train this bird to do, for their amusement, what it habitually does for its own living.   Of this we shall have more to say later, when dealing with this particular branch of sport in which the rabbit is concerned.

One more bird deserves a passing notice in this connection.   The brown owl, known also as the tawny or wood owl, although preying usually on rats, mice, field voles, and small birds, is by no means averse to taking a young rabbit when it gets the chance.   But probably only the very small ones fall victims in this way, for it has neither the strength nor the weight sufficient to hold a heavy old buck or doe in the frantic efforts which it would make to escape.

When dealing on a preceding page with the subject of the maternal instinct which prompts an old rabbit to attack an intruder in defence of its young (p. 20), mention was incidentally made of the way in which a carrion crow was driven away when on the point of killing a tiny rabbit, which had incautiously wandered too far from the parental burrow, and it is probable that most of the crow family, and particularly the carrion crow and the raven, are cunning enough, now and then, to secure a young rabbit for supper, in spite of the vigilance of its courageous parent.

Rabbits, like other animals, have their ailments ; and few people probably would suspect the variety of diseases to which they are subject. Amongst the chief causes of disease are over-stocking, breeding in-and-in, and living and feeding on tainted and unwholesome ground. To these causes may be attributed enteric or typhoid fever and tuberculosis—maladies which sometimes manifest themselves with such virulence as to give rise to a general and alarming mortality.

Occasionally rabbits are found lying dead in all directions. This may arise from 'scouring' produced by a flush of grass after a dry season, or (if fed) by giving too much green food, or food that is too wet with dew or rain upon it. But sometimes rabbits will die when about half grown, which, on examination, will be found to have been suffering from an enlarged abdomen and tuberculous liver. It is a true saying that *prevention is better than cure*, and this especially holds good in the present case, for cure is out of the question ; the only rational treatment being the extirpation and removal of the diseased animals, and the introduction of fresh, healthy stock when the ground, after a dressing of salt and lime, has recovered its pristine freshness, and become wholesome.

Salt, though not a direct 'plant food,' has an important indirect effect upon the potash, lime, and magnesia in the soil, affecting their decomposition, and rendering them in an available condition to be taken up by the roots ; in other words, salt acts as a purveyor to the plants. Lime, on the other hand, is a direct 'plant food,' and indirectly it acts in many important ways, neutralising poisonous acids, and causing the decomposition of organic matter. The application of these manures, therefore, will be found to increase the amount of herbage considerably. The land should be first dressed with gas lime, say, three tons to the acre, and subsequently with salt, say 2 cwt.

Quite distinct from tuberculous liver is the disease known as 'pulmonary tuberculosis,' caused by the presence in the lungs of a parasitic worm, *Strongylus commutatus* (*Filaria pulmonalis* of Frölich). Hares as well as rabbits are attacked in this way, but from the observations of M. Megnin it would appear to be less known in England than on the Continent.

Rabbits are also liable to be affected with large hydatids, or watery tumours, which usually appear on the hind quarters. These indicate the early stage of a tape-worm, which is matured in the intestinal canal of the dog. Fortunately this does not affect the human species, so that when gamekeepers puncture such tumours, and send the rabbits to market, there is no danger to be apprehended by the consumer. Should, however, a rabbit thus affected be eaten, or partly eaten, by a dog, the germ will develop into a mature tape-worm, whose eggs, when perfect, are voided by the dog, and swallowed on the herbage eaten by rabbits. They then produce, not tape-worms, but the original hydatid, which again gives rise to a repetition of this series of changes.

The researches of the late Dr. Spencer Cobbold, and other helminthologists, have demonstrated the curious fact that tape worms and other entozoa found in the intestines of men and animals, pass the early stages of their existence in a larval form in the flesh of animals on which man feeds ; and, seeing how instrumental a dog may become in spreading disease of this kind, it is obviously of importance to prevent useless curs from wandering about the fields and coverts, lest, by feeding on infected rabbits, they finally infect others in their turn. We may appropriately quote here Dr. Cobbold's salutary caution to owners of sporting dogs. 'Sportsmen,' he says, 'who care for the welfare of their dogs should never allow them to devour the entrails of hares captured in the field. In the county of Norfolk I have myself witnessed this piece of carelessness on the part of keepers, and have ventured to remonstrate accordingly. Almost every hare (and the same may be said of full-grown rabbits) harbours, within its abdominal cavity, a larval parasite (*Cænurus pisiformis*), which, when swallowed by the dog, becomes transformed into a tape-worm (*Tænia serrata*) varying from two to three feet in length. In harriers and greyhounds this serrated tape-worm is very abundant, but in other dogs it is comparatively rare.' This significant fact should not be lost sight of.

If we examine a rabbit thus affected we find the hydatid or tumour, sometimes as big as a filbert, surrounded by a couple of investing membranes, the outer one belonging to the unfortunate host, the inner one being part of the hydatid itself. On opening the body cavity, it will be found to contain amongst the viscera hundreds of the smaller pisiform species of hydatid which, when eaten by dogs, becomes the

E

Tænia serrata. These hydatids, which, as above
stated, are produced from the minute eggs of the
tape-worm voided by the dog and swallowed with
herbage by the rabbit, cause the emaciation and
ultimately the death of the unfortunate animal they
infest.

Those who may desire to pursue this subject
further should consult a paper, by Dr. C. W. Stiles,
' On the Tape-worms of Hares and Rabbits,' printed
in the ' Proceedings of the United States National
Museum' (vol. xix. 1896, pp. 145–235), in which will
be found two plates illustrating tape-worms of the
rabbit. Dr. T. S. Palmer, in a Report on the Rabbits of
the United States, observes:[1] 'Many persons have a
prejudice against eating rabbits because at certain
seasons they are infested with parasites, or because the
flesh is supposed to be " strong." This prejudice, however, is entirely unfounded. The parasites of the rabbit
are not injurious to man ; furthermore, the ticks and
warbles occur at a season when the rabbit should not
be killed for game, while the tape-worm can only
develop in certain of the lower animals, as, for example, in the dog.'

[1] U.S. Department of Agriculture, Bulletin No. 8 (1896).

CHAPTER II

THE WARREN

In its original sense the word 'warren,' old French *warenne* and *varenne*, later *garenne*, mediæval English (*e.g.* in 'Piers Plowman') *wareine*, and Low Latin *warenna*, signified a preserve in general, and came subsequently to be restricted to an enclosure especially set apart for coneys and hares. 'Coney-close' ('Paston Letters,' iv. 426) had the same meaning, and 'coney-garth' (Palsgrave), 'garth' signifying in the North of England, according to Ray, a small enclosure adjoining a house. Halliwell, who also gives this meaning,[1] adds that of a 'warren.' In almost every county in England, as remarked by the editor of the 'Promptorium Parvulorum,' near to ancient dwelling-places the name 'Coneygare,' 'Conigree,' or 'Coneygarth' occurs, and various conjectures have

---

[1] *Dict. Archaic and Prov. Words.*

been made respecting its derivation, which, however, is sufficiently obvious.[1]

From 'warren' we get 'warrener,' Latin *warinarius* ('Prompt. Parv.') corrupted into the surname Warner.

When considering the precise meaning of the word 'warren' at the present day, we have to distinguish between what is indicated by the legal expression 'free warren' and what is popularly known as a warren. The latter is merely an enclosed field, or piece of down-land, in which coneys and hares are reared. Any one may have such a place, and it would be protected under the Larceny Act (24 & 25 Vict. c. 96, s. 17); but its possession gives none of the rights of 'free warren,' which can only be derived by a grant from the Crown—a privilege no longer extended[2]—or by prescription or long use, which presupposes or implies a grant.

The right of 'free warren' is a franchise in that sense of the word which implies an exemption from ordinary rule, and attached to its original creation was the condition of keeping others off the land. It confers upon the grantee the exclusive right to kill or

[1] See Hartshorne's observations on names of places in *Salopia Antiqua*, p. 258.
[2] Woolrych, *Game Laws*, p. 26.

take 'beasts and fowls of warren' within certain limits, and to prevent others from killing or taking them, even on lands of which they are the freeholders.

As to what species are, or were, included amongst 'beasts and fowls of warren' there is some little conflict of opinion. Manwood, in his 'Treatise and Discourse of the Lawes of the Forrest' (the first edition of which was printed in black letter in 1598), asserts that this expression included the hare, the coney, the pheasant and the partridge, 'and none other,' justifying this definition from the 'Register of Writs,' and 'Book of Entries,' which show that in every case in which an action was brought by any grantee of free warren against a trespasser, the statement of claim invariably ran 'et lepores, cuniculos, phasianos, et perdices cepit et asportavit.' He was quite clear, therefore, that the 'beasts and fowls of warren' were limited to these four species. In Coke's report of Sir Francis Barrington's case (8 Rep. 138) the same definition is given ; but in his treatise upon Littleton the Lord Chief Justice enlarges considerably, as though a much longer list of species was allowed in his day. He says : 'There be both beasts and fowls of the warren ; beasts, as hares, coneys and roes (called in records *capreoli*) ; fowls of

two sorts, viz. *terrestres* and *aquatiles* ; *terrestres* of
two sorts, *silvestres* and *campestres* ; *campestres*, as
partridge, rail, quail, &c. ; *silvestres*, as pheasant and
woodcock, &c. ; *aquatiles*, as mallard, herne, &c.'
The validity of this definition was questioned in a
celebrated case, the ' Duke of Devonshire *v.* Lodge '
(7 B. and C. 36), in which the defendant was charged
with shooting grouse on land over which the plaintiff
claimed the right of free warren. The shooting was
admitted, and the only question to be decided by the
Court was whether a grouse was a bird of warren.
Manwood being considered a higher authority on the
Forest Laws than Coke, it was held that a grouse is
not a bird of warren. Lord Tenterden's judgment
in this case puts the matter very tersely and clearly.
He remarked, ' The franchise of free warren is of great
antiquity, and very singular in its nature. It gives a
property in wild animals (animals *feræ naturæ*), and
that property may be claimed in the land of another,
to the exclusion of the owner of the land. Such a
right ought not to be extended by argument and
inference to any animal not clearly within it. . . .'
Relying, therefore, upon Manwood's doctrine, he
non-suited the plaintiff.

A right of free warren differs from the right of
forest, chase or park in that the latter implies the

ownership of the soil; while the former is an incorporeal right, and does not necessarily imply any right to the soil, the reason being that a franchise of warren may be claimed by prescription, but land cannot, the title by prescription being only applicable to incorporeal hereditaments.[1] The right of free warren has usually been granted to the lord of a manor over the demesne lands of the manor,[2] *i.e.* such lands as are in the lord's own hands, though sometimes over Crown lands when it is a warren in gross. As to the privileges of an owner of a free warren, he may not only prosecute a trespasser who is in pursuit of beasts and fowls of warren, whether he be a stranger in the locality, or a tenant of lands within the limits of the free warren, but he may also kill any dogs found hunting in his warren, whether they are doing damage at the time or not. His rights, moreover, are expressly safeguarded by Section 8 of the principal Game Act (1 & 2 Will. IV., cap. 32). Free warren is not forfeited by non-user, and it is important to note that an occupier of land within the limits of a free warren is not entitled, under the Ground Game Act of 1880, to kill rabbits on the land in his occupation,

---

[1] Earl Beauchamp *v.* Winn, L.R. 6 H.L. 223.

[2] The words of the ancient grant were, 'quod ipse et heredes sui habeant *liberam warrenam* in omnibus *dominicis terris* suis in A. in comitatu B.'—Manwood, fol. 23.

as he would otherwise be at liberty to do were no
such franchise claimed by the lord of the manor.
This point was made clear by the case of 'Lord
Carnarvon *v.* Clarkson.' The question arose under
Section 5 of the Ground Game Act, which provides
that ' Nothing in the Act shall affect any special right
of killing or taking ground game to which any person *other than the landlord*, lessor, or occupier may
have become entitled before the passing of this Act
by *virtue of any franchise*, charter, or Act of Parliament.' Lord Carnarvon was lord of the manor of
Highclere, Hampshire, and at the same time a person
'other than the landlord,' and he claimed the franchise of free warren over the land of which Mr.
Clarkson was the occupier. This deprived Mr.
Clarkson of the benefit of the Statute, and the operation of this saving clause (Sect. 5) is curious ; for it
enabled Lord Carnarvon to do as 'lord of the manor'
what the Act expressly prevents him from doing as
'owner ;' in other words, the lord of the manor is
thus placed in a better position than the landlord.
A report of the case will be found in *The Field* of
May 18, 1895. It did not come into court, but
was settled practically by the occupier admitting
himself to be mistaken in his interpretation of the
Statute.

The lord of a manor with a grant of free warren generally may place his coneys wherever he pleases, either within the manor, or elsewhere, and not even a commoner can interfere with him. Under the altered conditions, however, which regulate sport, and the requirements of agriculturists at the present day, it is doubtful whether any one so circumstanced would think of asserting his strict legal right to such an extent as this. If he has a warren by prescription, he may use his right according to the accustomed privilege, but not further. If he has it by grant, he may go to the extent of his grant, but not beyond ; and in these cases, according to Serjeant Woolrych ('Game Laws,' p. 31), it seems to be the same whether there be or not any difference between 'warren' and 'free warren,' *i.e.* whether the limited right should be termed 'warren,' and the more enlarged franchise 'free warren.' On the other hand, no action will lie against a lord of the manor for keeping coneys on land over which he has a right of warren.

Any owner of a warren, whether enclosed or not, may prosecute a trespasser for killing rabbits or hares there. The remedy is specially provided by Section 17 of the Larceny Act (24 & 25 Vict. c. 96), which runs as follows :—'Whosoever shall unlawfully and wilfully, between the expiration of the first hour after sunset and the beginning of the last hour before sunrise, take or kill any hare or rabbit in any warren or ground lawfully used for the breeding or keeping of hares or rabbits,[1] whether the same be enclosed or not, shall be guilty of a misdemeanour : and whosoever shall unlawfully and wilfully, between the beginning of the last hour before sunrise and the expiration of the first hour after sunset, take or kill any hare or rabbit in any such warren or ground, or shall at any time set or use therein any snare or engine for the taking of hares or rabbits, shall, on conviction thereof before a Justice of the Peace, forfeit and pay such sum of money not exceeding five pounds as to the Justice shall seem meet.'

We shall have occasion later on to refer to further points of law when dealing with other portions of the general subject.

Having now briefly glanced at the subject of

[1] The ground must be used *mainly* for that purpose, for if only a few rabbits are kept, for example, in a rick-yard mainly used for other purposes, this offence would not be committed (*Regina* v. *Garratt*, 6 C. & P. 369). In the case of *Bevan* v. *Hopkinson* (34 L.T. 142), where B. was caught with rabbits at night in a field forming part of a farm over which H. had the right of shooting, the Justices found as a fact that this field was *not* a warren within the meaning of this Act, and convicted B. of night poaching, under 9 Geo. IV. c. 69, s. 1.

warrens from the legal aspect, and having thus obtained, as I trust, a clear conception of the meaning
of the term in its twofold signification, we may proceed to consider some of the more important details
connected with the formation and general management of a warren.

It will be gathered from what has been already
stated, that a warren may be unenclosed, and of considerable extent, as, for instance, when on sandhills
by the sea, or upon open down-land ; or it may be
of comparatively small size, say, forty or fifty acres,
and enclosed for greater protection. The larger the
feeding area, of course, the better, and the less need
is there for enclosure, unless cattle or sheep are
allowed to graze in the vicinity, since the rabbits have
less incentive for straying, and the very openness of
the ground gives greater security, for it makes it
more difficult for an enemy to approach unseen. It
is naturally otherwise when the warren is confined
to a comparatively small area, for to prevent them
from straying in search of 'fresh woods and pastures
new,' it becomes necessary to confine them within
stone walls or a rabbit-proof fence, which may serve
the double purpose of preventing the rabbits from
getting out, and other creatures from getting in.

The question of soil is of the first importance, for

upon the suitability or otherwise of the ground selected the success of the undertaking will, in a great measure, depend. A stiff clay soil, for example, is very undesirable ; nor can rabbits burrow properly where the ground is too rocky. What suits them best is a light sandy soil, and peaty ground, as on moorlands, will do well enough provided it does not lie so low as to become flooded after heavy rain, in which case, of course, the young rabbits would be drowned, and the older ones driven out of house and home. ' Burrows in flat ground,' says Mr. Simpson of Wortley, 'are the cause of serious loss, for during heavy and sudden rains, the holes become reservoirs into which the water quickly drains, and drowns the young rabbits.' In an old warren in his neighbourhood, which is level—and where the rabbits are forced to burrow on the flat surface—not a year passes without serious loss from drowning. Two years in succession it was reckoned that nearly the whole of the first brood was lost. After a storm every burrow would be full of water, and numbers of very young rabbits might be seen lying dead, floated out at the mouths of the holes.

Hilly, sloping, or undulating ground, with a light soil, is what one would naturally select if available ; failing this, heavy land may be treated in such a way

as to counteract, in a great measure, its natural dis-
advantages. For example, on a clay soil, wherein
rabbits evince a disinclination to burrow, their comfort may be secured by artificially throwing up
mounds of earth on the surface, and sowing them
with grass seed. Mr. Simpson recommends that
such mounds should be thrown up in parallel lines,
about 100 yards apart. They are easily made,
and will cost about 9*d.* per cubic yard to throw up.
They may be about four yards wide, and three feet
above the ground line at the apex. In making them,
the following directions should be given to the
labourers : ' Set out a circular piece of ground, four
yards wide, and round that a ring a yard wide. Dig
the soil out of the outer ring, and throw it roughly
into the centre, gradually making a conical heap,
with holes here and there, formed by rearing up on
end two large sods, and placing them gable-wise.
Above this the earth should be piled loosely till the
desired height is attained.'

With this incentive to begin digging on their
own account, the rabbits will soon complete these
excavations, and form regular burrows. Mr. Simpson
notes the importance of having them so made at first,
that the rabbits can find shelter in them at once,
and when fresh stock is introduced into a warren, the

animals should always be put into the burrows on arrival. Strange rabbits, he says, if put down in the open, will wander round the outskirts at the fence, and will lie and sulk for some time before they find a burrow ; whereas when put into the burrows they stick to them, and are sooner at home. When a mound is finished, it should slope with a curve to the bottom of the trench out of which the soil has been dug, where it will be about five yards in diameter. Should the soil or subsoil be of such a nature as to cause the rain water and drainings from the heap to stand in the trench, grips or drains should be made to the nearest field drain or outlet to let the water off.

The object of having these mounds of moderate size, and about 100 yards apart, is to ensure the rabbits cropping the pasture regularly in every part, from beginning to end of the season, and a greater distance than 100 yards apart is not desirable, as experience will soon prove. Besides, rabbits breed best in small colonies. If there be objections to the mounds being so close, they may be put wider apart, but they must be proportionately larger. Two men will throw the heaps up in a very short time, and should the ground come to be used for any other purpose, they can be quickly levelled down again.[1]

[1] See some very practical remarks on 'Artificial Rabbit Burrows' in *The Field* of March 18, 1893.

The success of a warren, however, depends on the burrows being distributed regularly over the pasture. If this be attended to the rabbits will eat all the grass, and be proportionately prolific : otherwise loss is certain.

It should be observed that this excellent advice of Mr. Simpson is chiefly applicable to warrens in which rabbits are bred for the market, and are taken by means of ferrets and nets, or with a specially constructed 'trap-fence.' Where the warren is laid out for the purpose of shooting, something more than this is required. For example, it will be found a good plan to throw down heaps of faggots, which afford excellent temporary shelter from wind and rain. Rabbits love to lie under them, snug and dry, and previous to a day's shooting the stacks may easily be ferretted, and the rabbits, when driven out, prevented from returning by surrounding the stacks with wire-netting, which can be afterwards removed.

From what has been already stated, under the heading of Disease (p. 46), it will be seen that it is of great importance that the ground should not become stale or tainted, if a healthy stock of rabbits is to be maintained ; and to prevent this one can hardly do better than follow the advice of Mr. Lloyd Price, whose experience in such matters is well known. He recommends that portions of the ground should be fenced with wire-netting, and crops of clover, oats, or beans grown within the enclosure. When these have been carried, or partly so, the wire-netting may be removed, and the rabbits allowed access to this reserved ground. By changing the position of these plots the rabbits get access periodically to fresh untainted ground, and thrive accordingly.

Mr. Simpson doubts the probability of the land becoming what has been termed 'rabbit-sick' if it is dressed—as he has practised annually—with a good dressing of gas lime and salt.[1] It may be imagined that this offensive-smelling manure would be injurious to the rabbits, and prevent their feeding on the ground treated with it. This supposition, the author maintains, is a fallacy, as, so far from the gas lime being repulsive to rabbits, they will even make their burrows in a heap of it.

He attributes the failure of many of the old warrens to the fact that thousands of rabbits have been removed from them year after year, and perhaps forty to fifty thousand pounds weight of meat and bones taken away annually, and nothing put back. His estimate of the number of rabbits that can be kept on an acre of grass, properly manured with gas

[1] As to this, see under heading 'Disease,' p. 47.

lime and salt, is from fifty to a hundred per year.
On the larger inclosed warren at Wortley Hall, which
is only partially stocked (77 acres of park land with
some covert adjoining), the average number of rabbits
taken up each year has been 3,000, which is about
forty rabbits per acre, and a good deal of grass is left
uneaten. It is not to be inferred from this, however,
that a warren half the size would produce the same
number of rabbits to the acre. No doubt half the
number of acres will suffice to feed 3,000, but they
require space as well as food or their domestic
arrangements will be sadly interfered with. Over-
crowding means interference with the does when
suckling, and there ought to be room enough to
obviate their being disturbed, as they would be if there
were too many occupants of one burrow. If a warren
is to pay for maintaining there is no need to waste
half the food it will produce. This implies a loss.
If there is to be a profit, the area and the feed upon
it should be no greater than is actually required to
support the stock. The question how many rabbits
should go to the acre can only be answered in general
terms, for it is obvious that an acre in one county
may contain double the quantity of food found on
another where the soil and the nature of the vegeta-
tion may vary considerably.

It goes without saying that, where shooting is the object in view, the more natural covert there is upon a warren—in the shape of gorse, fern, heather, or tussocks of grass—the better, not only for the rabbits, but also for winged game, especially partridges and woodcock. Natural shelter of this sort is always attractive to the latter, and the enjoyment of a day's rabbit-shooting is always heightened by coming suddenly upon a covey that lies well in such ground or flushing (and, let us hope, bagging) an unexpected woodcock.

The amount of fencing which may be required to protect a warren adequately must depend wholly upon circumstances. The ground may be so situated as to be surrounded either wholly or in part by stone walls, which only require to be topped with wire to constitute an efficient rabbit-proof barrier. Where this is the case a considerable saving of expense may be effected ; for all that is needed, after stopping holes and crannies, is to surmount the wall with wire-netting, laid on sticks a yard long, in such a way as to slope inwards, and so prevent the rabbits from jumping out, the sticks being kept in their places by heavy stones, and earth rammed into the inter-stices.

Where no such boundary walls exist, one must

have recourse to fencing, the cost of which, according to Mr. Simpson, need not exceed one shilling per yard. For this outlay one may construct a fence which will keep in the rabbits, prevent their burrowing under or leaping over, and strong enough to turn cattle or ordinary trespassers. The fence is made with two sizes of wire-netting ; that at the bottom must be at least 18 in. wide, with $1\frac{1}{4}$ in. mesh, as a larger mesh lets through the younger rabbits, which do not return. The upper wirework is $2\frac{1}{2}$ ft. wide, with a $1\frac{1}{2}$ in. mesh. This wirework is supported by oak or larch posts, $5\frac{1}{2}$ ft. long, charred at the bottom. The netting is placed inside the posts, which are driven eighteen inches deep, a yard apart, so that they stand four feet out of the ground. Each piece of netting is folded so that part of it is horizontal ; six inches of the lower netting lies flat on the ground—this, it is found, prevents the rabbits burrowing under; and six inches of the upper netting, also, is turned in horizontally, and is supported by bolts and a wire, so as to prevent the rabbits running up and leaping over. The tops of the posts are secured by being connected with stout wire, either plain or barbed, the latter making it cattle proof. This wire is found to prevent the entrance of foxes.

Where sheep or cattle are allowed to graze on the

outside of a warren there is always a risk of their breaking down the wire-netting by pressing against it from the outside in their attempts to reach the herbage within, and some further precaution on this score may be necessary. To obviate this danger Mr. Lloyd Price recommends that short posts, standing a foot above the surface of the ground, should be driven in *outside* the warren fence, and about two feet away from it, and that a barbed wire should be run along the tops of them ; that is to say, at a height designed to catch the knee of an animal proceeding to examine the permanent fence with a view to offensive operations ; and when once any beast has had a taste of its quality, the low, inoffensive-looking wire is always avoided most carefully in future, thus saving the regular fence from much ill-usage in the shape of horning, rubbing, or other attacks. Of course, this little extra precaution adds to the expense, but it is an excellent safeguard.

If the warren is not intended to be shot over, but is merely maintained for the purpose of breeding rabbits for the market, they may be taken either by ferreting and netting, or by means of an ingenious contrivance designed by Mr. Simpson, and termed by him a ' rabbit trap-fence.' This is a long piece of wirework, as long as the covert to be worked, say, 50 or 100 yards. It is reared up and temporarily supported on its whole length with stakes, the bottom just touching the ground. Parallel to it another length of fencing is set up, the lower part of which projects inwards, and is supported by a number of pieces of loose stick, propping it up every twenty feet. When the rabbits come out to feed they run under the first netting, the lower part of which is open, but cannot pass the second ; and a man who is concealed at some distance pulls a galvanised wire, which upsets the whole of the sticks holding up the flap of wire, which consequently falls down, and as many as 500 rabbits have been caught at once between the two fences.

As there are probably many landowners who would prefer to lay out a warren on a less extensive plan than that advocated by Mr. Simpson, it may be well to quote here the experience of Mr. J. H. Leche on a warren of forty acres only, as described by him in *The Field* of February 24, 1894. He writes :—' The total acreage is about forty acres, of which seventeen is grass only, with no burrows on it; the remainder is young covert, about twenty years old. Part of that which is planted is sandy, and part clay subsoil; the open part is, generally speaking, strong soil. It was inclosed in April, 1893, and when we shot it, we killed

exactly 1,000 rabbits to six guns before luncheon.
Only seventy of these were killed in the open, and the
rest were killed crossing rides, in the part which is
wood. The wood is divided down the centre by a
broad grass ride, and there are eight cross rides. In
August and September 250 live rabbits were turned
into the warren which had not been bred there.
About October 1 (or three weeks before we shot) I
found the rabbits were very thin, and between then
and the time we shot they consumed about fifteen
loads of swedes, two bags of Indian corn, and two
trusses of best hay. Inferior hay is of no use;
rabbits will not eat it, or, if they do, it does them
very little good. The hay was placed under sheets
of corrugated iron, supported by four ordinary stakes.
By this means it was kept dry—a most important
thing to see to, for unless kept dry rabbits will scarcely
look at it. The swedes were grown on a piece of
land inside one of the coverts, which was ploughed
for the purpose, and, having the old turf in it, the
land required no manure of any kind. Since we shot
I have had every rabbit I could get hold of destroyed,
and I re-stocked the warren about the last week in
January. Altogether about 1,100 rabbits were killed.

'The open part of the warren is land worth, say,
1*l.* per acre to farm, and I have limed all the rough-

est part, applying about five tons to the acre, and since then it has been moss harrowed. The part which is eaten off bare will be dressed with a light application of dissolved bones, also the main ride down the centre of the wood.

'You cannot have a large stock of rabbits, year after year, on a small warren like this, without periodically doing something to help the land upon which you keep them ; but, by clearing the ground for three months every year, and occasionally liming, I believe it to be quite possible ; and I see no reason why a rabbit warren should not pay if you do not shoot the rabbits, but watch the markets, and either trap or net them.'

Trapped or snared rabbits should realise, say, 2s. 9d. a couple ; shot ones 2s. 8d. a couple ; taking out, of course, any badly shot, and sending only good sound rabbits to market.

It is important to bear in mind the difference between farming a warren for profit, and laying it out for sporting purposes. In the former case you may have four or five times as many rabbits to the acre as can be maintained in the latter case. Mr. Simpson, referring to the former, writes :—'I know, and am sure, that fifty rabbits can be produced to an acre of fair pasture ; but I should expect a hundred.'[1]

[1] *The Field*, March 14, 1896. This opinion is confirmed by another writer in *The Field* of November 9, 1889.

Another correspondent wrote :—'In a season like the past summer, when grass was abundant, our ground would have produced at least 150 rabbits to the acre. As it is, fifty to the acre have not consumed one quarter of the pasture. Large tracts of it are still untouched. So rank was the herbage in August and September that about thirty cattle had to be turned in to help to eat it down.'

On the other hand, rabbit warrens which are used for sporting purposes only, and are not shot until November, will not bear ten rabbits to the acre without serious damage. Warrens which are farmed, and snared or netted from the end of September onward, are not so unremunerative ; but the gun should be discarded until the very last.

As to the effect of rabbits on pasture, a practical observer, after three years' experience, has remarked that 'a rabbit puts nothing back into the ground, though he extracts the utmost from it. He leaves little manure on the grass, and his droppings have little manurial value.' This is not the case where rabbits are farmed in hutches, and the hutches are periodically shifted. Major Morant, in his 'Profitable Rabbit Farming,' writes :—'It is generally believed that the manure of rabbits injures the ground; but this is a great mistake : it is as beneficial as that of sheep.' The question is : Do rabbits in hutches which are frequently moved, injure or benefit pasture? The answer to this is supplied by a writer in *The Field* of January 11, 1896, who remarks :—' I have had 300 rabbits in hutches on a pasture in front of my house, and the hutches were moved twice a week. The effect on the pasture was simply marvellous—quite equal to the effect of sheep. The manure from fixed hutches was sold to farmers at seven shillings for a small cartload, and the demand was far in excess of the supply.'

As to the profit to be made out of rabbit-farming, that must depend upon various circumstances—acreage, and proportionate cost of fencing, rent, and keepers' wages, cost of winter feeding (old hay, swedes, Indian corn, &c.), cost of dressing with gaslime and salt where the impoverished herbage requires it (see p. 47), and so forth.

The result obtained by Mr. Simpson, in Yorkshire, seems to have been very different from that obtained by Mr. Elwes, in Gloucestershire, where, if we are not mistaken, the rabbit land is poor pasture on the oolite limestone, and not worth more than 5s. per acre, pastured, moreover, with sheep to its fullest capacity. Mr. Elwes is no believer in the profits supposed to be made out of rabbit warrens, or in the possibility of keeping fifty or even a hundred rabbits to the acre for a series of years.[1] As Mr. Simpson, however, has demonstrated that it can be done, and has answered Mr. Elwes's objections,[2] it is evident that no general rule can be laid down, and that results must in every case depend upon the conditions under which the warren is formed, and the nature of the ground selected for the purpose.

Whether warrens deteriorate in their productive qualities in course of time, or not, is a disputed question, to which Mr. Lloyd Price, however, has given a decided answer. He asserts that if properly managed, a warren does *not* deteriorate, but continues its production per acre without cessation, subject only to the chance of very inclement and wet seasons. After fifteen years' experience, he found, in 1894, that the same land which, under sheep, yielded 2s. 6d. per acre, produced 18s. per acre when under rabbits.

All these subjects are discussed in his book ' Rabbits for Profit, and Rabbits for Powder ;' and are dealt with also by Mr. Simpson and Major Morant in their respective treatises above mentioned.

The limited space at disposal here precludes our discussing them at greater length. To these sources of information, therefore, we may refer the reader

[1] *The Field*, March 7, 1896.   [2] *Ibid.* March 14, 1896.

A WARRENER OF THE OLDEN TIME

who is desirous of going into greater detail than we
have been enabled to do in the foregoing pages.

The duties of a warrener at the present day are
somewhat different from what they used to be when
Sam Alken, that prince of sporting artists, portrayed
the good old-fashioned sort which we see depicted
on the opposite plate—a facsimile reproduction from
his drawing. On looking at it, one cannot but
admire the sturdy and weather-beaten form accustomed to work single-handed in all weathers, and the
'scratch pack' by which he is accompanied, any
member of which is able to catch and hold the
heaviest buck rabbit, or tackle a stoat or polecat with
the slightest encouragement.

A century ago the wold warreners were wont to
catch their rabbits with 'fold-nets,' with 'spring nets,'
and with 'tipes,' or tip-traps. The 'fold-nets' were
set about midnight, between the burrows and the
feeding ground, the rabbits being driven in by dogs,
and kept enclosed in the fold until morning. The
warrener would drive towards the net with the wind
if possible ; a side wind would do, but nothing could
be done if the wind blew over the net towards the
outlying rabbits. This is also very noticeable when
catching hares with 'hays,' and arises from their very
keen sense of smell.

A rough-coated dog, called a lurcher, smaller and shorter than a greyhound, but somewhat of the same build, was often used to drive the rabbits towards the nets, and with the warrener's training was rendered extremely useful, for he was taught to watch the rabbits out at feed, when he would dart on them without the least noise, and carry them one by one to his master, who would wait in some convenient spot to receive them.

The 'spring net' was generally laid round a hay-stack or other object likely to attract rabbits in numbers.

The 'tipe,' or tip-trap, was a kind of cistern, with a lid nicely balanced on a pin through its centre, over which the rabbits were led through a narrow meuse. The lid was at first bolted so as not to tip up, and the rabbits were allowed to go through the meuse, and pass over it for some nights until they got accustomed to the run. The bolt was then withdrawn, and one after another they would be tipped into the cistern, from which, in due time, they were 'culled' by the warrener, who killed the fat ones, and turned the others out to improve. By this means, at the end of the season, the bucks and does were sorted, one of the former being considered sufficient for six or seven of the latter, and the nearer they could be brought to this proportion, the greater was the produce of young expected. Great precaution was needed in using these traps, for should too many rabbits be admitted at once, or allowed to remain for too many hours in the closed cistern, numbers would die from heat and suffocation, and the carcasses would be spoiled. The cisterns, therefore, had to be carefully watched, and when the required number was caught the meuse was stopped, and the trap-door fastened. In this way it was possible to take five or six hundred rabbits in a single night.

The trap-fence adopted by Mr. Simpson, and already described (p. 68), is an improvement on this method, and has much to recommend it; but the majority of warreners at the present day are content to get their rabbits by trapping, ferreting, netting, and digging out. A rabbit thus caught always fetches a better price at market than one which has been shot, for the skin is then uninjured, and there are no ugly wounds, nor extravasation of blood beneath the skin, to spoil the appearance of the meat.

When treating of the natural enemies of the rabbit (pp. 39–44) we took occasion to allude briefly to the stoat, weasel, polecat, fox, badger, rat, and cat. The warrener who knows his business will not tolerate the presence of any of these on the warren if he can help it. The three first-named are best caught in one of two ways : either in an iron trap (or gin) over which a bait is suspended, or in a box-trap. In the former case the trap should be set close to the wall or fence which surrounds the warren, and on the outside, not only to avoid catching a rabbit, but because a stoat or weasel, in an attempt to get in, will run a long way on the outside of the fence and quite close to it. The bait should be suspended at a little height above the trap, so as to cause the animal to rear up in its attempt to reach it, and, by overbalancing, to drop on the plate of the trap and so get caught. The trap in this case should always be set with the catch next the wall, for, if placed the other way, the intended victim might not be heavy enough to weigh down the lever and so spring the trap. The entrails of a rabbit or fowl make as good a bait as can be used, the smell being attractive for a long distance. If this cannot be procured immediately it is wanted, and a bit of butcher's meat has to be substituted, it may be made more enticing by scenting it with musk, or oil of rhodium, or aniseed. This will be attractive also to rats and cats ; but of them we shall have more to say later. A trap should never be re-set in the same place after a kill, and should be handled as little as possible, and with gloves on, for these wild creatures are wonderfully quick in detecting the taint of the human hand.

The second mode of catching stoats and weasels is by means of a good-sized box-trap, not *single*, like a mouse-trap, but *double*—that is, to open at both ends ; and it may be either baited with a strong smelling bait, or have an unbaited gin set in the middle of it. A stoat or weasel is more likely to enter a box-trap if he can see daylight through it than if it be closed at one end like a mouse-trap. For this reason it will often answer well to place a gin in a culvert or drain, or set one (unbaited) at each end. A modification of this plan is to set a few slates or tiles in a sloping position, and in a row against the foot of a wall with an unbaited gin behind them on the ground. We have caught many a rat by this plan, and it is equally efficacious for weasels. For our own part, however, we would not ruthlessly trap and kill every weasel and stoat on the warren. A few of these animals, if left to their own devices, are useful in checking too abundant an increase of rabbits, and, indirectly, improving the stock by killing the weakly ones, which are more easily captured.

The utility of the weasel, in checking the devastation of field mice, has never been more clearly established than by the evidence which was tendered to the Committee appointed by the Board of Agriculture to inquire into the plague of field voles in Scotland, in 1892. In the Minutes of Evidence appended to the Report of this Committee, issued in 1893, will be found numerous statements, elicited by cross-examination of the witnesses, which tend to prove beyond doubt that the weasel is the natural enemy of field mice, and that no greater mistake could be made than to destroy the former where the latter are numerous, or threatening to become so. The field mice did incalculable mischief in Scotland by eating up the grass on the sheep runs, thereby causing the sheep to starve, and consequently to depreciate in value, while the failure of lambs was so serious as to cause heavy loss to the farmers. It is easy to foresee what would be the effect in a rabbit warren if it were to be similarly over-run by field mice, and there were no weasels to keep them in check.

From a huntsman's point of view, of course, foxes are best left alone—that is, if the warren is in a hunting country. They must eat to live, and being fond of rabbits, they will take these where they can get them easily, and pay the less attention to pheasants and other game. Should the warren, however, happen to be situated in sandhills near the sea, on unrideable moorland, in rocky ground, or in a country unvisited by fox-hounds, the warrener probably will not be much troubled with conscientious scruples in regard to the destruction of foxes, when, if they should prove to be too numerous, a poisoned bait, an iron trap, or a well-timed shot, will put a stop to the too rapid consumption of coneys.

Wandering cats, as every gamekeeper knows to his cost, are an unmitigated nuisance, and when they take to feeding on young rabbits, of which they are very fond, the warrener will have to put a stop to such proceedings as soon as possible. The quickest way to get rid of them is to shoot them, although, by the expenditure of a little more time and trouble, they may be cleared off by poisoning, or trapping. In wet weather cats will walk along the wall of a plantation, when it will be found a good plan to hollow out a coping stone and set a round trap in it.

Rats, also, have to be reckoned with, and in warrens are best got rid of by ferreting ; but by digging out and bolting them, a good many may be killed with the aid of the 'scratch pack' above referred to. The ferret, however, is so indissolubly associated with the rabbit, and so important an ally of the warrener, as to deserve special treatment in the next chapter.

G

CHAPTER III

FERRETING

WHEN the Romans introduced the rabbit into Italy they introduced the custom of hunting it with ferrets ;[1] and when they carried the same animal into Britain they imported the same custom with it. The great reason for the Roman introduction of the former animal into both was the pleasure which they took in hunting it with the latter. The Britons adopted what the Romans practised, and have transmitted to us, their successors, the Roman-Spanish hunt, and the Roman-Spanish name for the animal employed in it ; denominating the latter *Viverra*, in Welsh *Guivaer*, and in Irish *Firead*, or *Ferret*.

The early use of ferrets is made apparent from several sources of information. They were employed by Genghis Khan[2] in his imperial hunting circle at Termed in 1221, and are mentioned by the Emperor

[1] Pliny, *Hist. Nat.* lib. x. cap. 21.

[2] Ranking, *Historical Researches on the Sports of the Mongols and Romans* (1826), p. 33.

Frederick II. of Germany in 1245, amongst the animals used for hunting.[1]

So long ago as 1390 in Richard II.'s time a statute was passed prohibiting anyone from keeping or using greyhounds and *fyrets* who had not lands or tenements of the annual value of 40s. Both the *fychew* and the *fyret* are mentioned in 'Thystorye of Reynard the Foxe,' as printed by Caxton in 1481,[2] and in the 'Book of St. Albans' in 1486. In the 'Household Book of Lord William Howard of Naworth,' several entries occur which clearly indicate the employment of ferrets and nets for taking rabbits in Cumberland in 1621.[3]

Many writers have asserted that the ferret is a native of Africa, but the statement lacks confirmation from the fact that the animal has not been met with in a wild state in any part of that continent, where, however, other kinds of weasels exist. The better opinion is that the ferret is merely a domesticated variety of the polecat, with which it is frequently crossed for the purpose of improving the breed. There are positively no cranial, dental, or other struc-

[1] *De arte Venandi*, ed. Schneider, 1788, tome i. p. 3.

[2] Ed. Percy Society, p. 109.

[3] This volume is of much interest not only to antiquaries but also to sportsmen from the numerous allusions which it contains to blackgame, roedeer, woodcock, wild-fowl, salmon, &c. It was printed for the Surtees Society in 1878.

tural characters by which they can be distinguished, and the brown variety of the ferret is so like a polecat that it might well be mistaken for one. The appearance of a ferret is too well known to require description. With most wild animals the result of domestication is to increase their size and weight. With the ferret it is otherwise. The average weight of a male polecat is $2\frac{3}{4}$ lb., and of a female $1\frac{3}{4}$ lb. ; no such weights have ever been recorded for ferrets. The reason for this is no doubt to be found in the different conditions of existence to which the two animals are subjected ; confinement, want of fresh air, insufficient exercise, and want of warm animal food operate in the case of the ferret to produce an undersized, weakly, and spiritless progeny.

There can be no doubt that the more the treatment of ferrets approximates to the natural conditions of life, the hardier and better they will be, and this is the secret of success in their management. Instead of keeping them in a shed or outhouse, in a small hutch with a bedding of musty straw, saturated with wet and dirt, so productive of 'foot rot,' 'sweat,' and other diseases, with a small saucer of sour milk and a piece of tainted meat on which to live or starve, they should be kept, at all events for the greater part of the year, as much as possible in the open air.

If there is sufficient ground at disposal, a good method of keeping ferrets is to make an enclosure with planks set edgewise one above another, and held in proper position with stakes. The sides should be high enough to keep the ferrets in, and low enough to be stepped over when necessary for the purpose of cleaning out the hutches. The latter should be off the damp ground, and have small openings for the animals to go in and out, so that they may be comfortable and warm at night. They are thus enabled during the fine weather to gallop about the enclosure, bask in the sun, and breathe pure air, the result being that they remain lively and vigorous, and free from disease.

The most suitable food is bread and milk, or porridge (not too wet, and by no means allowed to become sour), varied occasionally with fresh meat in the shape of small birds, mice, young rats, or a piece of freshly killed and warm rabbit. This should be tied to a staple with a bit of string to prevent the ferrets from dragging it into their sleeping place and thus soiling the bedding. They should never be fed in the morning of the day on which they are to be used, but on being brought home should have a good supper as soon as possible, and should then be allowed to go to sleep.

On commencing to keep ferrets it is of course important to get hold of healthy stock, and the inexperienced beginner who is no judge of points must be guided by the advice of friends, or rely upon a good breeder. The sexes are distinguished as 'hob' (or 'dog') and 'jill,' and should be kept apart except at pairing time, when they may run together for a day or two. Ferrets will breed twice a year, but usually only once, in summer. The period of gestation lasts six weeks, and the young, usually six or seven in number, are born blind, and do not open their eyes for a month. Within a week of their being expected, the sleeping compartment of the mother should be closed, after making up a fresh bed, and not be reopened for the next five or six weeks ; for if disturbed before then the mother will probably destroy them.

When they first show themselves outside their sleeping box and begin to feed with the 'jill,' they will require careful attention and must be fed three or four times a day. When about ten weeks old, if looking strong and well, they may be put in another hutch.

As above stated the ferret will breed readily with the wild polecat, and there can be no doubt that a cross with the latter improves the breed materially, for the young are stronger in constitution, and work quicker and longer than ordinary ferrets, which after two years get slow and lazy. The half-bred progeny while growing up require more handling and more work than ordinary ferrets do, or they get shy of being picked up. The second cross is perhaps the best for general purposes, although the first cross produces capital ratworkers round stacks where agility is indispensable.

On the subject of muzzling and coping much difference of opinion prevails. The writer favours the view that a ferret should never be muzzled, and it is doubtful whether coping ought not also to be dispensed with, as it clearly should be when hunting rats. A coped ferret cannot kill a rabbit, but will scratch and worry it in the attempt to do so. A rabbit will bolt much sooner from a ferret that is free. If the ferret be worked on a line, care should be taken that there are no roots of trees or rocks underground, or the line will soon get fast, and occasion much trouble.

It will not do to handle ferrets while they are quite young, or the old one will very likely destroy them. It will be time enough to handle them when half grown, and it should then be done boldly without snatching the hand away, or it will provoke them to bite.

As to the mode of transport nothing can be more

objectionable than the time-honoured 'bag' which most keepers and warreners use to save themselves trouble. Carried in this, a ferret is never at rest, and is so cramped and worried as to lose half its energy for work. Should the bag get wet, as is often the case, either from a downpour of rain or from being laid down on wet grass, the ferret is made thoroughly miserable, and will take an early opportunity of 'laying up' in the first comfortable burrow it enters. The best way to carry ferrets about is in a small wooden box with a rope handle. It should be perfectly dry, and one half may be partitioned off, with a small hole for ingress and egress, and be littered down with fine shavings of willow, or deal; or, failing either of these, straw. Carried about in a box like this, they will get rest, and be much more lively when wanted for use.

In 'entering' young ferrets it is a good plan to let them run with the mother, who will soon initiate them in working a rabbit burrow. If they are slow to follow her down a hole, she can be used with a line and pulled back from time to time to entice them forward. It is as well to give a young ferret its first chance in a burrow where it will be sure to find a rabbit, as in a short sandy hole, and to reward it with a kill. Nor should it be worked too long at first, but be allowed an occasional rest. If a rabbit is bolted and shot, it should be pegged down outside the hole, so that the ferret on coming out may find it at once, and be rewarded. Should a ferret 'lay up' or remain a long time in a hole, another ferret on a line should be run in, and the truant dug out; hence the desirability of choosing an easy place to begin with when entering young ferrets.

A rabbit will sometimes decline to bolt, and will be killed in a burrow; the ferret will then have a gorge and 'lay up.' In that case the plan is to leave a boy to watch the burrow, or to set a box-trap just outside, and visit it next morning.

An old ferret that has been used constantly in the same neighbourhood, will learn to find its way home like a dog. Instances of this ' homing instinct,' as it has been termed, have been frequently commented on, and reported. See *The Field*, January 25, and February 1 and 8, 1873; January 23 and 30, 1886; March 17, 1888.

The late Dr. G. J. Romanes, in his book on ' Animal Instinct,'[1] states that on one occasion while ferreting rabbits he lost a ferret about a mile from home, and that some days afterwards the animal returned. He adds: 'I once kept a ferret as a

[1] *Internat. Sci. Series*, vol. xli. second edition, 1882.

domestic pet. He was a very large specimen, and
my sister taught him a number of tricks such as
begging for food, which he did quite as well and
patiently as any terrier, leaping over sticks, &c. He
became a very affectionate animal, delighting much in
being petted and following like a dog when taken out
for a walk. He would, however, only follow those
persons whom he well knew. That his memory was
exceedingly good was shown by the fact that after an
absence of many months during which he was never
required to beg, or to perform any of his tricks, he
went through all his paces perfectly the first time that
we again tried him.'

It is perhaps not generally known that other
animals of the weasel kind, besides the ferret, are
capable of being tamed, and make very pretty and
engaging pets.

Mademoiselle de Faister described her tame
weasel to Buffon as playing with her fingers like a
kitten, jumping on her head and neck, and if she
presented her hands at the distance of three feet, it
jumped into them without ever missing. It distinguished her voice amidst twenty people, and sprang
over everybody to get at her. She found it impossible
to open a drawer or a box, or even to look at a paper
without his examining it also. If she took up a paper

or book, and looked attentively at it, the weasel immediately ran upon her hand, and surveyed with an inquisitive air whatever she happened to hold.

But to return to the ferret. We have already referred to the importance of preserving cleanliness in the hutches if ferrets are to be kept in health. The various diseases by which they may be attacked result chiefly from inattention to this point. Distemper or sweat, red mange or eczema, and foot-rot generally arise from the animals being kept in a dirty condition or in a damp situation.

Three or four times a year the hutches should be washed out and disinfected with Condy's fluid, and then whitewashed inside. This is the best way to keep them clean and sweet; at the same time, of course, attention must be paid to the bedding, which should never be allowed to remain wet or musty, nor should the ferrets be allowed to carry their food into their sleeping place, for any that is left there will soon turn sour, and become injurious.

Ferrets do not require to be fed often; once in twenty-four hours should suffice; for if given food more frequently they are liable to get fat and lazy, instead of being (as they should be) keen and active.

It is not easy to compress into a few pages all the points upon which it might be desirable to touch in connection with the management and working of ferrets, but this perhaps is not altogether necessary, for several books written by experts have been devoted entirely to this subject. It will suffice to give a few hints that will be found useful in practice.

When handling a ferret take it under the forelegs, above the ribs, and if it struggles, let its forelegs go through the fingers. Ferrets do not like to be held below the ribs. Do not handle a 'jill' ferret about to have a litter. The young ones should not be allowed to run with the old male, or 'hob,' until they can use their teeth to defend themselves. By calling them to their food at meal-times they soon learn to obey a whistle like a dog, and give no trouble on being picked up. Moreover they can then be let out much more frequently to run about, and with this indulgence are less likely to contract foot-rot.

A ferret trained in this way will work a hedgerow from end to end by himself, affording his owner shot after shot if he stands well out in the open.

Bells are of no use. They only alarm the rabbits, and are not heard in deep burrows.

Nothing makes a rabbit lie so close as the sound of men tramping and talking, and terriers yapping overhead ; a terrier used for ferreting should be mute. Never talk loud, therefore, while ferreting, and *never stand in front of a hole*, but always away from it, or the rabbit will not bolt. Where possible choose the holes over which the wind is blowing towards you, for a rabbit's sense of smell and hearing is very acute.

When the ferret issues from a burrow do not be in a hurry to pick it up, but let it get a few feet from the hole, or it may perhaps dodge back and refuse to come out again. Should this happen the truant may be enticed out by throwing down a dead rabbit at the mouth of the burrow.

Everyone who has had experience of rabbit-shooting must have remarked a fact which indicates either a want of intelligence in rabbits or an inability to learn by experience. When alarmed they run for their burrows, and when they reach them, instead of entering, they very frequently squat down to watch the enemy. Now, although they well know the distance at which it is safe to allow a man to approach with a gun, excess of curiosity, or a mistaken feeling of security in being so near their homes, induces the animals to allow him to approach within easy shooting distance. Yet that in other respects rabbits can learn by experience must be evident to all who are accustomed to shoot with ferrets. From burrows which have not been much ferreted, rabbits will bolt soon after the ferret is put in ; but this is not the case where rabbits have had previous experience of the association between ferrets and sportsmen. Rather than bolt under such circumstances, and so face the known danger of the waiting gun, rabbits will often allow themselves to be torn with the ferret's claws and teeth. This is the case no matter how silently operations may be conducted; the mere fact of a ferret entering their burrow seems to be enough to assure the rabbits that sportsmen are waiting for them outside.

FERRETING

CHAPTER IV

SHOOTING

EVERY lover of the gun will admit that he owes a debt of gratitude to the ubiquitous rabbit, and its extinction, which is not merely threatened by existing legislation, but in some places has been actually accomplished, will be a matter of regret for everyone but the agriculturist who possesses no sporting instincts. The absence of a close time and the knowledge that rabbits may be shot all the year round—though we have ventured to protest against killing them after the expiration of the shooting season when the does are suckling their young (see pp. 10, 11)—afford many persons an excuse for a day's sport when game cannot be killed; while the fact that there are a great many shooters whose means do not permit of their renting partridge-ground or pheasant-coverts, justifies their regarding the rabbit as especially created for their particular diversion. Truly, a day's covert-shooting without rabbits would be deprived of very much of its enjoyment, and a day with spaniels or terriers on a furze-clad common under similar circumstances would be rendered practically abortive. The supply of 'rabbit-pie' would be dependent upon the commonplace efforts of the warrener, and half the charm of a day with the gun in the open would be gone.

Who does not remember with feelings of pleasure the day when, allowed for the first time to carry a gun in company, his earliest efforts were directed towards circumventing and slaying a 'bunny'? He was sure of a find, he could choose his distance, and pick his shot. Not only was the target a sufficiently large one, but, unlike the whirring partridge, it travelled at a speed sufficiently moderate to give time to aim, and with a little practice the young sportsman soon got into the way of handling his gun properly, and swinging it well forward with the happiest result.

The schoolboy home for the Christmas holidays and taken out with a gun and ferret has good cause to be grateful for the lessons taught him by the wily rabbit, and if from inheritance, or choice, he possesses the true sporting instinct, he will in after days look with satisfaction upon his earliest efforts at rabbit-shooting. Many will be the 'misses,' perhaps, and few the 'hits,' but there is sport even in missing, and the day at length will come when the nerves are sufficiently steady and the aim sufficiently good to justify his being one of a shooting party under the guidance of an older hand.

Not until the autumn leaves have commenced to fall, and briar and bramble have begun to look thin in the coverts, can rabbit-shooting be prosecuted with any advantage. The undergrowth is still too thick for any game to move through it rapidly, and the rabbits can only creep about, scarcely showing themselves, and affording but poor chances of a shot across the rides. For as long as there is covert they will stick to it, and until the underwood gets thinner, they will double back and defy the most strenuous efforts of beaters to get them out.

Nevertheless, long before the big woods can be beaten, rabbits will afford some amusement in the hedgerows amongst old pastures, if worked with one or two good spaniels and a gun on either side to shoot those that can be forced to bolt. Again, when the corn is ripe, and the reaping machine is at work, going round and round the field, laying swathe after swathe, and gradually reducing the area of standing grain, the rabbits instead of bolting will work towards the centre, availing themselves to the last of the little shelter that remains, until the men, at the bidding of

H

the sportsmen, stop the horses, and constituting themselves beaters for the occasion, put out rabbit after rabbit towards the expectant gunners. Thus pressed they will make in fine style for the nearest hedgerow until turned head over heels by a well-directed charge of No. 6 shot. In this way a score of rabbits may often be killed in half an hour by a single gun, while if two guns are posted on opposite sides, the fun will be all the merrier while it lasts. The farmer will be well pleased, and the harvesters too, if they receive, as they should do, a rabbit or two apiece for their pains.

Pending the advent of covert-shooting, there are few pleasanter ways of spending an afternoon than by shooting rabbits on a furze-clad common, either with dogs or beaters, or both. The surroundings are particularly exhilarating. The weather is usually splendid, everyone is in a good humour, the common is all aglow with the golden furze on which here and there the stonechat sits and clacks his disapproval at the invasion of his haunts. The merry spaniels eager to begin can scarce control their excitement, and the mere sight of a rabbit elicits from them a veritable yell of delight. With difficulty they are restrained until the guns are properly posted, each commanding a ride cut through the thick furze, with one behind the beaters to take toll of any rabbits that may go back. The word is given to advance, and the dogs at once dash in. It is marvellous how they face the furze, and how untiringly they work throughout a hot afternoon. The young shooter who leaves the ride and essays to follow them in quest of an open space in which he thinks to get plenty of shooting, is soon taught to wonder what sort of skin a dog possesses, when his own is lacerated at every step, and his knees above the gaiters are turned to pincushions. But the irritation of the moment is forgotten in the excitement of the sport. A spaniel gives tongue on his right, a sudden movement of the furze is seen, a great brown hare slips out in front of him and, cantering some way down the ride to his left, disappears on the other side before he has time to recover from his surprise. He has quite forgotten to ask his host whether hares are to be shot or not, so thinking it is perhaps rather too early in the season, he has prudently refrained from firing, and is pleased to be told later that he has done right.

A shot from a neighbour's gun followed by the squeal of a rabbit tells him that the latter was very nearly missed, but one of the spaniels has got hold of it, and it is speedily put out of pain. Another shot, and another, serve to announce that the sport has now fairly started. Rabbits are everywhere on the move, working towards the rides down or across which they scamper in their haste to avoid the dogs, yet giving (if they only knew it) to the sportsmen a better chance of killing them than if they had remained in the furze. The dogs are in ecstasies of delight—the place is full of rabbits, and their pursuers are perpetually changing the quarry. But steadily the line is advancing, and every rabbit must, if possible, go forward, or break to the right or left across a ride in which a gun is posted. A dozen yards from where we stand, a little brown head peeps out, a large dark eye regards us wistfully, the owner of which is evidently speculating on his chance of crossing the ride in safety; his ears twitch nervously; he 'bucks up,' and we instinctively grasp the gun-stock tighter in the expectation of an immediate shot. But his discretion overcomes his valour; we see the whisk of a white tail, and in an instant he has turned back and is lost to sight in the furze from which we fondly hoped he was about to bolt. Whilst marking the spot and wondering whether he will reappear (for a beater is not far off), another little brown face peers out, this time lower down the ride, and in an instant a brown streak crossing within easy range offers so quick a

RABBIT-SHOOTING IN THE OPEN

chance, that we are scarcely surprised to see the turf receive the bulk of the charge a few inches behind the mark. So close a shave was it, however, that we mechanically walk to the spot for the purpose of seeing precisely how far we were out in our calculation, when, much to our satisfaction, we find the rabbit lying stone dead within a foot or two of the edge of the ride—a few outside pellets have done their work, and the career of that merry 'bunter' is ended. 'Guns to the right of us, guns to the left of us' proclaim a continuation of the fray. A sudden yelp, another in a higher key, and then a chorus of spaniels as the entire pack sweep down a ride in full pursuit of a rabbit, and so close behind it that shooting is out of the question. A sudden wrench to the left, the leading dog overshoots the mark, and the second dog with the rabbit in his mouth falls headlong into the furze, the others tumbling head over heels upon them, a brown and white mass of struggling, writhing forms. The rabbit is with difficulty taken from them, and thrown down on the ride where a goodly row is already laid out and marks the progress that has been made. In the parallel ride a similar row is in evidence, amongst them a black one, and also a nice young leveret which someone has mistaken for a sandy rabbit. We are now approaching the end of the first strip of furze, and as the beaters close up and the rabbits that have gone forward are getting towards their last place of refuge, the guns are having a lively time of it. 'Rabbit on the right!' shouts an excited beater; 'Rabbit coming out to the left!' yells another. Shot after shot rings out, and many a grey form turns a somersault on the green ride, followed instantly by a spaniel, which after mouthing it for a few seconds, and wagging his tail, turns into the furze again to find another.

And here we may remark upon the advantage of having one or two spaniels that can retrieve. It often happens that a wounded rabbit crawls away into thick furze, where without the aid of a dog it is difficult to find. The stuff is often so dense that it is impossible to see the surface of the ground, and many a rabbit hit hard, or, as sometimes happens, killed by the dogs, is left behind for want of one that can bring it out. On this account spaniels are preferable to terriers, and being less excitable, they are not given to wander so far from the guns. Their longer coats too serve them in good stead in the sharp-pointed furze-brakes which they are compelled to face.

As dogs and beaters draw nearer together, and the excitement increases, great care has to be exercised by the guns lest some unlucky spaniel, more impetuous than the rest, should receive a charge of shot not intended for him. And here the schoolboy should be told to take the cartridges from his gun, and watch the cool procedure of the older hands. He should be taught always to 'play for safety,' and never to risk a shot where there is the least danger of striking anything but the object aimed at. It is so easy to kill a rabbit and a dog with one shot, or miss a rabbit and pepper a beater, that the wonder is it does not happen oftener. The beaters themselves often get so excited as to create an element of danger by the excitement they cause in others, especially in young sportsmen, who for want of experience have not yet acquired the nerve and self-control so essential when rapid firing is going on. The danger arising from this cause is even greater in covert-shooting, owing to the fact that the beaters work towards the guns, and are nearest to them when the heaviest shooting takes place. It is then that accidents are more likely to occur. In pure thoughtlessness we have seen a young sportsman, aye, and a middle-aged one too, who ought to have known better, fire at a rabbit in covert when the advancing line of beaters was within range of his gun. This is bad enough when the object fired at is on the ground, as in the case of a rabbit or hare, but it is ten times worse when the shooter recklessly fires at a low-flying pheasant before it has left the covert, and while at an elevation calculated to drop the shot in the face of some unfortunate beater. We have seen this happen more than once, and have shudderingly awaited the result, expecting instantly to hear a cry of pain from some recipient of the dropping pellets, an anticipation which we regret to state has been occasionally fulfilled. Had the positions of guest and host been reversed we should have had no hesitation in rating the delinquent soundly in the hearing of the other guns, and warning him that a repetition of his offence would mean disqualification for the rest of the day, and the non-receipt of any future invitation.

The responsibilities of a shooting host are greater than many seem to consider. Not only is the life of the game both furred and feathered in his hands, but he is responsible to a great extent for the lives of the beaters, who are placed in considerable peril when called upon to advance towards reckless shooters, and his first care should be to reduce the danger of the situation to a minimum.

Let us quit the furze-clad common where we left the shooting party with their spaniels at the end of their first beat—for one beat is very much like another—and take a glimpse at the very different scene which presents itself when the leaves are falling in the big woods and pheasants claim more attention than the rabbits, although the latter constitute very often an important item in the day's account.

The *modus operandi* is altogether different. It is true that in the earlier part of the season, when the underwood is still pretty thick, and patches of fern and bramble afford strongholds for game that can scarcely be invaded without the help of dogs, spaniels are extremely useful, for they can creep through places where a beater would be 'hung up,' and push forward many a rabbit which would otherwise be certain to 'go back.' In such covert, also, the wily woodcock will often lie so close without rising as to allow a beater to walk past him, while his scent will betray him at once to the questing spaniel, who will very soon have him on the wing. On this account a team of close-hunting spaniels will be found invaluable early in the season, especially if broken, as they should be, to hunt always within range of the guns, and to drop to hand when bidden.

Later on, when the woods get more open, and the beaters can move more freely, the spaniels may be dispensed with, and in their place two or three steady retrievers may be employed, which should never leave the heels of their employers until bidden to 'hie lost.' They should then be allowed to work entirely under the direction of their owners, and not be confused by directions given by other people, who are often too prone to tell a dog what to do instead of leaving him alone to his own devices, which are much more likely to lead him right if he is a good bred one, and has been properly handled. Nor should the impetuous young sportsman who sees his winged pheasant or dead rabbit in the mouth of a retriever be in a hurry to take it from him. The dog should be allowed to carry it straight back to the man who sent him, and whom he knows. Not only is this much better for the dog, which is then not confused, but it will prove a considerable saving of time in the course of a day's shooting, especially if the object be a big bag and there be much ground to get over.

It is not our intention to attempt here anything like directions for covert-shooting, for not only would this be superfluous in the eyes of readers who know a great deal more about it than the writer, but it would be out of place in a volume designed to treat exclusively of the rabbit. Moreover, this part of the subject will be found fully dealt with by masters of the craft in the volumes which have already appeared on the ' Pheasant ' and ' Hare.'

We may content ourselves with a few observations

which have reference more especially to rabbit-shooting in covert, and are designed to give some insight
into that particular phase of sport. Such prelimin-
aries as the placing of 'stops,' and the pegging down
of low nets along the rides where the woods are of
considerable extent, and have to be beaten in sections,
may be taken for granted. It goes without saying
that inattention to such matters as these will have an
important bearing on the results of a day's covert-
shooting.

Both hares and rabbits are possessed of a keen
sense of hearing, and no sooner do they hear the
'tapping' of the beaters, or the bark of a spaniel,
than they at once begin to move forward, and seldom
pause until they are beyond the reach of such disturbing sounds. The forward guns then get plenty of
shooting, and the campaign is generally opened with
a good show of rabbits. The instinct of the pheasant
on the other hand induces him to crouch on hearing
a noise, and to seek safety, in the first instance at all
events, by trusting to the protective coloration of his
natural surroundings rather than to flight. As the
beaters come nearer, he will run forward a little way,
and crouch again, repeating this manœuvre as long
as it is feasible, until he is suddenly scared by the
appearance of a dog or beater, or until he has run up

to the edge of a ride in which one or more guns are posted. Then it is time to take wing, and if the nearest gun knows his business, the fate of that cock pheasant is sealed.

It is otherwise with rabbits. They will cross a ride at lightning speed as if aware that their lives depend upon it ; pausing only on the edge before crossing, if they happen to come out unexpectedly near to the gun. And, indeed, their safety often depends upon their crossing as near the gun as possible ; for no one with any regard to the condition of game when picked up will care to risk blowing a rabbit to pieces at such close quarters.

Where the stuff is very thick, rabbits will often linger on the edge of a ride until the beaters are almost upon them, and 'the fun then becomes fast and furious.' Three or four rabbits may be seen crossing at the same time, and it often happens that on a cry of 'Rabbit for'ard!' the shooter's attention is directed so closely to the ground in front of him, that he misses a good chance at a cock pheasant which skims noiselessly overhead while he is 'otherwise engaged.'

The variety of shots afforded by rabbits in covert is best known to those who have tried to hit them, and many a keen shooter has discovered, by the

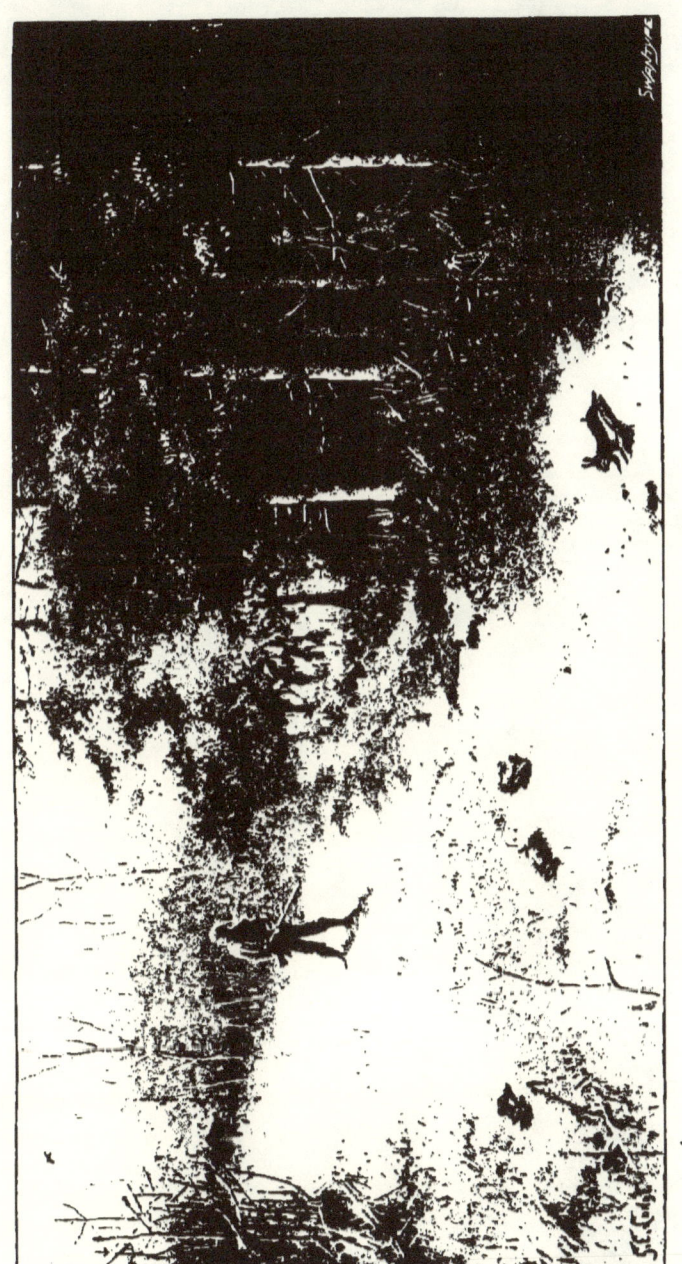

RABBIT-SHOOTING IN COVERT

number of empty cartridge cases, how easy they are
to miss. The secret of success lies in holding well
forward, and swinging the gun ahead as the trigger is
pulled. This is especially the case when rabbits are
crossing a narrow ride, when it becomes necessary to
shoot not 'where they are,' but 'where they will be'
by the time the charge is delivered.

And here we may remark on the advantage of
light loads in a long day's shooting. It is frequently
forgotten that the majority of shots in covert-shooting
are made at a distance under thirty yards, and a full
charge of three drachms of black powder, or the equiva-
lent in nitro-compounds, with $1\frac{1}{8}$ oz. or $1\frac{1}{4}$ oz. of shot,
is not only unnecessary but unadvisable. With $2\frac{3}{4}$
drachms and 1 oz. of shot the gunner will not only kill
his game well, but will do so with greater comfort to
himself; for under these conditions there will be less
recoil, no sore shoulder, and no headache to complain
of at the end of the day, while the rabbits will not
present the unsightly appearance which they do when
'plastered' at short ranges with a heavier charge.

In some of the more remote country districts
beagles are extensively used for rabbit-shooting, and
more especially is this the case in the southern
counties. Where rabbits are numerous, the coverts
small, or where hares are plentiful, beagles are not a

success; but in the big straggling Sussex woodlands that once formed part of extensive forests, the sport is frequently indulged in.   In these localities, after the regular season is finished there are still a few rabbits to be killed down, and an opportunity is afforded to give the farmers and their friends a day's rabbit-shooting.   The employment of an army of beaters to drive the rabbits to the guns would be expensive, and therefore beagles take the place of human beaters. Many of the farmers keep a beagle or two, and frequently a man may be the possessor of a good hard-working dog, which secures his owner many an invitation to a day's rabbiting.   As a general rule the keeper is allowed to invite the guns, and he, as a matter of policy, asks first the tenants whose land adjoins his coverts and then a few others to make up the party, but invariably those farmers are first asked who are likely to suffer most damage from the depreda-tions of the rabbits.[1]

' The owner of a couple of good beagles is tolerably sure of some shooting during the season, and often

---

[1] For these remarks on rabbit-shooting with beagles we are indebted to a writer in *The Field*, who is evidently well qualified to deal with the subject, but who chooses to be anonymous.   We can say from experience in the county to which he refers, that his description is quite accurate, and on that account we prefer to quote his own words rather than paraphrase them.

dogs are borrowed from non-shooting men, who get a couple of rabbits as an acknowledgment for the use of their beagles.

The dogs may be of all colours and sizes, but they know their work, and are hardly likely to give much trouble unless they hit the line of a fox, or break away after a hare. In the latter case, however, they generally bring her back, and can then be stopped; but once on the line of a fox they will at times run for a couple of miles or so. The guns take up their positions in the most likely places, generally on a 'ride' where there is a clear view in front, or in an open glade where they can see to shoot for some distance in every direction. The beagles search every clump of brambles, and push through the decaying bracken and thick undergrowth, until at last we hear a whimper from one hound as he puts out a rabbit, followed by a burst of music as the others rush up on hearing him give tongue. The guns are able to tell in which direction the rabbit has gone as the cry of hounds approaches or retreats. Then comes a pause as they overrun the line, a doubtful note succeeds, which increases once more into a burst of melody as they hit off the scent, and push the rabbit along at top speed toward the guns. A flash of brown fur across the 'ride,' and a snapshot as it disappears in the brushwood is followed by silence as the beagles come up and find their quarry dead.

Soon another rabbit is found, and once more the wood re-echoes the cry of the hounds, broken by the quick report as a shot rings out, which, however, does not always mean the death of a rabbit. Sometimes the rabbit will come quietly dodging along through the brushwood, affording an easy pot shot ; but more frequently, especially when hard pressed, he dashes along at lightning speed. Occasionally hounds will succeed in killing a rabbit, or in driving him to ground. As a general rule, the burrows are ferreted a day or two before, and the holes either stopped up or 'paraffined' in order to make the rabbits lie out and afford more sport. Old hands at the sport can tell at once when the beagles get on the line of a hare, and then out comes the pipe, the gun is put down against a tree, and the shooter takes things coolly, until warned by the approaching music that the hare has circled round, and hounds are then stopped and encouraged to pursue their more legitimate sport. Needless to say, the beagles used for rabbit-shooting must not be gun-shy. It is seldom that they work long at a burrow when once a rabbit goes to ground—and in this respect they are greatly to be preferred to terriers, that will often half bury them-

selves in their endeavour to scratch out a rabbit. It
is absolutely necessary for the guns to remain perfectly quiet and not move about, otherwise rabbits
will not approach.'

It has been already remarked how materially
rabbits help to fill the bag in a day's covert-shooting,
and it may be added that they also go far to relieve
the monotony of continuously firing overhead shots
at pheasants. So well is their utility in this respect
recognised that, for some days before a big shoot, a
vast amount of trouble is taken to stop them out, and
insure their being found when wanted. To do this
properly will give employment for several days to the
keeper and his men, and requires no little skill and
judgment. On this subject we shall have something to
say in the next chapter, where we propose to consider
the various methods of trapping, snaring, netting, and
stopping out which are usually adopted where rabbits
are numerous.

Mr. Lloyd Price has made us acquainted with all
that pertains to a sporting warren, and in his excellent
little book on 'Rabbits for Profit and Rabbits for
Powder' has shown what extraordinary bags may be
made of rabbits only, when the ground is laid out
especially for their preservation, and attention is paid
to the proper way of 'showing them.'

I

He cites bags of 1,850, 2,500, and 1,650 rabbits
'killed in one day, only beating half the ground,' and
since the publication of his book these figures have
been considerably exceeded on his own ground at
Rhiwlas, North Wales. For instance, a party of nine
guns shooting there in 1883 killed 3,684 rabbits in a
single day, and on another day, in 1885, as many as
5,086. Of this last number no fewer than 920 were
shot by Lord de Grey. The next best bag of rabbits
made by a single gun was that of the late Sir Victor
Brooke, who, shooting in his own park at Colebrook,
Co. Fermanagh, in 1885, killed 740 rabbits in a
day to his own gun. He fired exactly 1,000 cartridges, and shot from his right shoulder for one half
of the day, and from his left the other half.

To show what may be done in this way upon a
comparatively small shooting, *The Field* of December 1, 1894, contained the announcement that on
the previous November 19, Mr. Charles Eley and a
friend, each shooting with two guns in a forty-acre
warren, on the East Bergholt Highlands Estate, killed
no fewer than 900 rabbits, or twenty-three to the acre.
With a large party and on a much larger acreage, one
of the most celebrated days at rabbits was that which
happened at Bradgate Park, Leicestershire, the seat
of Lord Stamford, where on a certain day in December,

1861, thirteen guns accounted for 3,333 rabbits besides twenty-six head of other game. The way in which the operations were carried out on this memorable occasion has been described by the park-keeper, Mr. J. B. Lucas, in the following terms:

'Being in the service of the late Earl of Stamford as park-keeper at Dunham Massey, one of my duties was to attend the large battues on his lordship's other estates. I kept account of the game killed, and assisted the late Mr. Reeves in the management of the beaters, &c., at Bradgate, from 1855 to 1865, which included the season in which the celebrated "threes" bag was made.

'The principal home of the rabbits was an extent of several hundred acres of hills and rocks, rough, poor ground, covered with fern, rushes, and coarse grass. A small herd of red deer existed in this part of the park, which was surrounded by a stone wall, six or seven feet high, built without mortar, in the manner usual on Charnwood Forest. The deer park adjoined it on one side. Three walls, which were built at right angles to the main boundary wall, and ran out into the deer park, formed two inclosures, one about thirty acres, the other about forty acres. Holes were made, and fitted with wooden doors, at intervals along the main wall, so that the rabbits could be allowed to feed in the deer park at pleasure. They were never allowed to establish burrows in the two inclosures named, and as there was plenty of fern and rough grass in them, there was no lack of covert for shooting purposes.

'A good many rabbits were bred in another part of the deer park. To get at these, a portion of the best feeding ground was kept free from burrows. The same tactics were pursued inside the warren. Large patches of ground alongside the wall were set apart, the fern mown down at times to improve the grass, and all holes dug out. The rabbits were not allowed to feed on these patches and inclosures for a few days before the day of shooting, and great was the anxiety of all concerned when the night for the " pitch " arrived. This was, of course, the night before the appointed shooting day, and the bag depended on the wind and weather being favourable. Everything was kept as quiet as possible inside the park and warren, and as soon as the proper moment had come, when the rabbits were supposed to be well on the feed (this varied with circumstances), the doors in the wall were shut and locked, and long nets of the usual square-meshed stop pattern were set between the burrows and feeding patches. Sometimes the whole thing was a failure. Thick fog or heavy rain will keep rabbits at home effectually. When the 'pitch' was successful

the shooting was very pretty, and by no means easy.
The rough ground was always well covered with long
grass and fern, so that by the time the guns were
posted and at work the rabbits were seated all over
their allotted area.

'In the first inclosure 808 rabbits were shot in
twenty-three minutes on the "threes" day. The year
previous, 2,103 were killed over the whole beat in one
day.' [1]

Not unconnected with 'big bags' is the subject of
'odd shots,' for it is only natural on occasions when
more than the ordinary amount of shooting takes place
that some of the shots should be unusual ones. Two
rabbits at a shot would not be a remarkable performance in a warren, or on ground where rabbits have
been previously stopped out ; but two rabbits with
each barrel, or four at a double shot, is a feat which
is hardly likely to be performed often. Yet such an
achievement is described in *The Field* of July 14,
1894.

In October, 1888, a sportsman in the neighbourhood of Ripon, walking over a rough grass field, kicked
up and shot a rabbit at twenty-five yards distance.
To his surprise he found that he had killed a hare by
the same shot, her 'form' being directly in the line of

---

[1] *The Field*, April 19, 1884.

fire.   Only a foot separated the two as they lay dead.
A similar thing happened at Beverley in September,
1890, except that the order was reversed.   The shooter
fired at a hare and killed it, when immediately a rabbit
was seen to leap up a few yards further and tumble
over dead.

Two instances of an unseen rabbit being killed
when a grouse was shot at, occurred at Strathardle in
the autumn of 1890—one on August 20, when the
grouse was killed, and on being picked up a rabbit
was found kicking close by ; the other on September 22, when the grouse was missed and a rabbit
came rolling down the brae.   In December, 1888, Mr.
Alfred Ware, while rabbit-shooting on his father's
warren on Dartmoor, fired at a rabbit crossing a bog.
On going to pick it up, he found he had also killed a
jack-snipe.   On examination the snipe was found to
be lying just where the bulk of the charge had struck
the ground.   Probably other instances of the kind will
occur to our readers as having happened within their
own knowledge.

One of the most curious episodes in rabbit-shooting
which has fallen within the experience of the writer,
occurred some years ago in Sussex, during a day's
rabbiting with beagles.   We were shooting a 'hanger'
under the hill, into which the beagles had driven a lot

of outlying rabbits from under the juniper bushes on the downs above. And rare sport did they afford, for, pressed by the dogs, they made straight down hill for the covert immediately below them, into which they fell rather than ran, unless stopped halfway by a charge of shot which ended their career. This did not always happen, for a downhill shot at right-angles is one of the most difficult with a fast rabbit, since the gun has not only to be swung a good way in front, but also dipped, and one is very apt to shoot over the mark. We had followed the survivors down, and forming line at one end of the 'hanger' with a gun above and below, and a third inside with the dogs, we began slowly to advance. The writer was the lowest gun on the left, in a rough field across which innumerable 'runs' indicated the presence of lots of rabbits in the covert. Presently the gun inside shouted, 'Rabbit out on the left!' and in an instant, sure enough, a rabbit showed on the bank, paused for an instant, jumped the ditch, and raced across the field within a very few yards of the outside gun. So close was he, in fact, that he was given a little 'law,' and when about twenty-five yards off the gun covered him. Before the trigger was touched, however, he suddenly turned a somersault and fell dead, as much to the astonishment of the writer as to that of the inside gun, who had jumped on the bank to see the result of the shot. He saw the gun go up, no smoke and no report, and yet the rabbit went head over heels. Well might he ask, ' What sort of gun do you call that ?' It was not until the owner of the gun stepped forth to pick up the rabbit that the mystery was solved. The rabbit on leaving the covert had taken to a well-worn ' run ' in which not far out some poacher had set a brass wire. Into this the rabbit had rushed full speed, and broken its neck.

Another phase of rabbit-shooting remains to be mentioned—-namely, rabbiting on the sand-hills and in the cliffs, the enjoyment of which depends rather on the remoteness of the situation, the picturesqueness of the surroundings, and the invigorating air which blows in from the sea, than upon the amount of shooting to be obtained. For it will often happen that rabbits on the coast-line may be plentiful enough, but from the nature of their haunts—which may be exposed sand-hills with innumerable burrows, or rugged cliffs full of holes and crannies—it is by no means easy to get within shot of them. They will often wait apparently with little or no concern until you are very nearly, though not quite, within range, and then, having admirably judged the distance at which they feel safe, will scuttle off to their burrows out of harm's way. Now and then, perhaps, you come unexpectedly upon a coney which, trusting to its protective coloration, has crouched amidst some sand-grass in the hope of escaping detection, and pays the usual penalty for his temerity; or peeping over a boulder cautiously, you spy a number out at feed, some of which are within shot of your ambush, and two of which you manage to secure. In another instant the ground, erstwhile teeming with life, is completely deserted; every rabbit has disappeared beneath the surface, and the only living creatures to be seen are a few wheatears which flit jerkily away, or a solitary ringed-plover which, after piping for some seconds on the ground, flies rapidly over the sand-hills and is lost to sight.

In such situations as this, and indeed on exposed ground of any extent, such as a warren, or open down-land where rabbits are plentiful but covert scarce, the weapon to use is not a 12-bore breechloader, but a small-bore rifle. Not only will this be found most effectual at rabbits beyond the ordinary range of a shot-gun, but it makes so much less noise that rabbits are not nearly so much scared by the report. The comparative lightness of a small-bore single rifle, and the rapidity with which it may be fired and reloaded when fitted with a modern ejector, makes it an extremely handy little weapon for the purpose in view. Moreover it affords the shooter no end of amusement, and a greater test of skill than a shot-gun ; for it is obviously more difficult to hit a rabbit with a small bullet at sixty or seventy yards than it is to stretch him out with an ounce of No. 6 shot at five-and-twenty.

As to the particular pattern to be recommended much difference of opinion prevails. During the months of May and June, 1895, a voluminous correspondence on this subject took place in the columns of *The Field*, from which it appeared that hardly two of the writers were agreed as to the requisites of a perfect rook and rabbit rifle. If they approved a particular bore, they differed as to whether the bullet should be conical or spherical, and if the former, whether it should be hollow-fronted or not. If they agreed upon these points, they differed in the choice of powder, or in the charge to be used. There seemed, however, to be a consensus of opinion that with a view to safety in an enclosed country the smaller the bore the better consistent with efficacy at fifty yards, and that other requisites are a flat trajectory, powder that may be as nearly as possible smokeless, noiseless, and non-fouling, and a bullet that by expansion on striking will reduce to a minimum the chance of a rabbit getting away.

Shooting without a rest, a fairly steady shot with an accurately sighted rifle should be able to put a bullet in a 3-in. circle at 50 yards, while with a rest of any kind a 2-in. circle at the same distance should be an easy mark. It would be beyond the scope of the present volume to enter upon a discussion of the comparative merits of all the modern rabbit rifles that are now upon the market, nor shall we attempt it. There are several so good of their kind that it would be no easy matter to choose between them.

So far as the writer's personal experience extends, he could not wish for a better weapon than Messrs. Hollands' ·250 hammerless ejector with hollow-fronted bullet for rabbits, and solid bullet for rooks. Tried on the target by an expert, its accuracy was undoubted, while its killing power when subsequently tested in a warren was all that could be desired.

As to powder for small-bore rifles, there is much to be said in favour of 'Amberite,' the advantages of which are absence of smoke, less noise (which enables one to get more shooting at rabbits on a·still evening) and less fouling than with black powder.

The less frequently a rifle requires wiping out the better, and for this purpose the best material is a bit of old flannel, torn up into strips three or four inches long, and either wound round the end of a brass

cleaning-rod, or tied to a piece of string and pulled
through after dropping the string down the barrel by
means of a small weight.

When shooting rabbits with a rifle, it is not a bad
plan to have a wattled hurdle put up here and there
in the warren or open ground where the rabbits lie
out, under cover of which they may be approached or
waited for within range. Their sense of smell and
hearing being very acute, they should always be
approached up wind. Another good plan is to sit up
in a tree, for by being above them they are less likely
to smell you. Success, of course, will in a great
measure depend on the skill of the shooter, coupled
perhaps with a certain amount of luck in getting shots
at short ranges. It is obvious that the most perfect
rabbit rifle in the world may become useless in the
hands of a man who tries to use it like a gun. An
experienced London gunmaker was of opinion that
30 per cent. of misses with a rabbit rifle might be
excused, but one who has made good trial of the ·250
asserts that · with hollow bullets and fairly good
shooting not more than 6 or 8 per cent. of rabbits hit
should escape. With solid bullets the percentage
would be greater. Much, of course, will depend on
the distance at which they are fired at. It is not
every bullet that proves fatal to a stricken coney. If

RABBIT-SHOOTING WITH A RIFLE

hit too far back, they will often drag themselves away towards a burrow and escape. For this reason we would not fire at a rabbit beyond eighty yards ; for at a greater distance than this a dog would not have time to run up and secure it before it reached a hole. Some experts advocate the retention of a ferret on a line in case of need, so that should a wounded rabbit go to ground, the ferret may be used to drag it out. It is well to bear in mind when shooting rabbits in this way, that the dead ones should be allowed to lie where they fall until it is time to go home ; for if you leave your ambush periodically to pick them up the chances of sport will be materially lessened.

As we have described some ' odd shots ' at rabbits with a shot-gun, we may mention one with a rifle that is worthy of record. It was reported in *The Field* of September 9, 1893. Mr. W. C. Pickering, of Rhewl House, Mostyn, Flintshire, shooting with one of the handy little rifles above referred to, fired at three rabbits in line and killed them all ; and, strange to say, on a subsequent occasion, so he said, he repeated the performance.

CHAPTER V

TRAPPING, SNARING, NETTING, AND BOLTING

By these terms are understood the various methods or devices usually employed for killing or capturing wild rabbits.   It is, of course, true that other creatures besides rabbits, to wit so-called ' vermin,' may be trapped, snared, or netted as occasion may require, but this does not at present concern us.

The best known form of trap for taking rabbits or vermin is the gin.   This word, as now commonly applied, is generally understood to mean an iron spring trap, though it did not always bear that signification. It is a very old word.   The author of the treatise on ' Fyshynge with an Angle,' printed in the second edition of the ' Book of St. Alban's,' 1496, alluding to the avocation of the fowler, saith ' many a gynne and many a snare he makyth.'   Shakespeare has employed

the word as if synonymous with the snare or springe
with which woodcocks and snipe are taken.

> Now is the woodcock near the gin.
>> *Twelfth Night*, Act ii. sc. 5.

and again :

> So strives the woodcock with the gin.
>> *Henry VI.* part 3, Act i. sc. 4.

Izaak Walton in the first chapter of his ' Complete
Angler,' 1653, alludes to 'the pleasure it is sometimes
with gins to betray the very vermin of the earth.'   In
this particular sense of ' trap ' or 'snare,' the word is
really Scandinavian, the Icelandic *ginna* meaning
to dupe or deceive.   The Middle English ' gin,' as
remarked by Professor Skeat, was employed in a
wider sense than that now used, and was in many
cases certainly a contraction of the French *engin* (Lat.
ingenium), a contrivance or piece of ingenuity.

At the present day, as every reader knows, it is
commonly restricted to an iron trap having two rows
of teeth set in such a manner that the teeth are forced
together by a spring when the animal to be captured
treads upon a small iron · plate which is concealed
by having some soil loosely sprinkled over it.[1]

---

[1] Of the cruelty inflicted by these traps we shall have something to say anon (p. 131).   It would have been well indeed
had the Ground Game Act entirely prohibited the use of them.

There are various patterns of gins, some of which are so clumsy and so badly constructed that they are of very little use. As an exception may be mentioned Burgess's Spring Trap, described and figured in *The Field* of March 26, 1887. One of the best we know is made by F. Lane, of Plymouth, in which the parts are so well fitted that with fair usage they will never break or wear out. It is specially commended by Mr. W. Carnegie, who, in his little book on ' Practical Trapping,' thus describes it :—

'Most gins are wholly made of iron, but this is not so, for zinc and copper are introduced. The spring, the most important part of the trap, is thoroughly well tempered and strong, but nevertheless easily pressed down when the trap is being set. The flap and catch, and other important parts in which most makers fail, are of copper, and do not wear away like iron, nor do they rust, which would clog the trap and prevent it acting. The plate is square with the four corners taken off, and is of zinc, being so fitted as to be level with the jaws when set. These latter are thick and rounded, the teeth fitting one into another, though not closely, a space of $\frac{1}{8}$ in. being left between. The teeth should on no account be sharp or pointed, as their being so tends to break the leg and cut the sinews, thus liberating the rabbit ; nor should the teeth be continued round the turn of the jaw. The superior finish and general quality of these traps make them rather dearer than the ordinary ones. They cost 1*s.* 9*d.* each, but a reduction is made if taken by the dozen.

'In order to prevent the rabbit when caught drawing the trap away, the back piece of the gin is furnished with a hole at the end through which a chain about a foot long is attached by means of an S hook. This chain should have about eight links with a swivel in the middle, and a ring of $1\frac{1}{4}$ in. diameter at the end. It is purchasable apart from the trap, and should be well tested, as the weakness will be found where least looked for, viz. in the swivel, and this should always be examined. The ring is for a stake which is driven into the ground to hold the trap. The best wood for this is ash, which should be cut in lengths of 18 in., and split, then rounded off to the required size, fitted tightly to the ring, driven on to within $1\frac{1}{2}$ in. from the top, and be overlapped by this part, which ought to be left unrounded as far as the ring comes.'

The best way to set a gin is to cut out a piece of the turf or soil, and place the trap so that the plate is on a level with the surface of the ground, and then sprinkle it over with loose soil. Unless this is done a rabbit will be certain to avoid it.

K

The number of traps required will of course depend upon the extent of ground and the abundance or scarcity of coneys. It is not advisable to put down all the traps at once, but to begin with a few, and keep on increasing the number each day until they are all in use.

Since the Ground Game Act of 1880 came into operation, it has become illegal for anyone except an owner in occupation of his own land to set gins anywhere except within the mouth of a burrow, on account of the risk if set aboveground of catching pheasants or partridges, foxes or hounds. On this account, therefore, the directions given in old books for setting traps in hedge-banks, under walls or fences, or in 'runs' across open fields, must now be disregarded.

In the words of the Act (43 & 44 Vict. cap. 47) 'no person shall, for the purpose of killing ground game, employ spring traps except in rabbits' holes.' It has been decided, however, by the Court of Queen's Bench (November 26, 1885), in the case of *Smith* v. *Hunt* that this section does not apply to owners occupying their own land.

The Act referred to is of such importance to those who are interested in rabbits, whether as owners, occupiers, or shooting tenants, that we propose in another chapter [1] to give a brief exposition of its pro-

[1] See Chapter VII.

visions, and deal with some of the vexed questions of construction which have arisen in respect of it, and have been authoritatively decided by courts of law. We shall then have occasion to say something more on the law relating to trapping.

Before dismissing the subject here, we would say a word or two on the score of humanity, for we take it that every reader who reflects at all on the matter must admit that trapping as ordinarily practised by game-keepers and professional rabbit-catchers has a detest-able element of cruelty in it which cannot be gainsaid. What greater barbarity, for example, can there be than to allow a poor frightened rabbit (or any other . animal for that matter) to remain for hours in an iron trap, struggling until exhausted, or possibly contriving to get away with the loss of a limb? The modifica-tions which have been suggested at various times to lessen the injury done by a trap, by covering the teeth with list or india-rubber, have not proved wholly successful, for this plan has been found to lessen the grip to such an extent as frequently to permit of the animal escaping. Much more humane and quite as efficacious as an instrument of death is the wire snare, so well known to gamekeepers and to poachers.

If properly made of fine brass wire, and adroitly set in a 'run,' it means speedy death to the first

unfortunate rabbit that get   nto it.   Snares
give   much   less   trouble t..an traps, a 1 are more
easily carried about.   Their construction, too, is very
simple.   All that is required are a few pegs about a
foot long with a hammer to drive them in, and a few
yards of the fine wire used for picture-hanging.   The
rest is merely manipulation.   Picture wire is found to
answer the purpose best because it remains in the
position in which it is set without kinking.   The peg
is sharpened at one end and has a hole bored through
the other.   Through this hole the wire fifteen inches
long is passed and tied.   With the other end a noose
is formed about three inches in diameter with a slip
knot which runs up the moment any pressure is made
on the noose.   The peg is driven well down into the
ground, and the wire is set at the height of a hand's
breadth above the surface.   The thing is simplicity
itself, and the art consists in setting it where it is
most likely to catch something.   How to discover
the most likely places can only be learnt by patient
observation of the rabbits' haunts and habits.   A
well-used 'run' should be selected in preference to
one that looks as if only just made, and the snare
should be set in or near the middle of it, and not at
either end, for a rabbit starts slowly, and not until he
has made up his mind to cross from one side of a

field to another will he put on pace enough to carry
him into th snare before he perceives it. It then
appears to him nothing more than a grass stalk leaning across the run, and the mistake is discovered
when it is too late.

From a humanitarian point of view the wire snare
is open to the objection that its victims generally
undergo a slow process of strangulation in their
efforts to get free, but this is not invariably the case,
for the speed at which a rabbit goes headlong into
a snare will often dislocate the neck. A so-called
' humane rabbit snare' has been devised which will
hold a rabbit without strangling it. This contrivance, which will be found described and figured
in *The Field* of December 19, 1891, is in fact a very
slight modification of the ordinary wire snare. It
merely requires a knot to be made in the wire in such
a position as to prevent its being drawn through the
loop beyond a certain point. In other words, the
noose when over the head slips up to a knot which
effectually prevents strangulation and yet holds the
rabbit firmly and securely. Consequently the animal
suffers no pain, and is simply tethered with the wire
round its neck until liberated. It may then be either
mercifully killed, or removed alive for liberation elsewhere if desired. We understand that hundreds of

rabbits have been caught in this way on the property of Mr. Lloyd Price at Rhiwlas, near Bala, and removed without pain from fields and gardens, where they were doing mischief, to the warren, where they were liberated uninjured.

Another humane way of catching rabbits in warrens by means of a pitfall has been already described (see p. 76).

During the month of September, 1894, a correspondence was carried on in *The Field* for some weeks on the subject of 'Humane Rabbit-traps,' and a particular trap so-called was recommended by Captain J. Dunbar Brander. Several correspondents, however, who experimented with it expressed unfavourable opinions, and although regarded by some as theoretically good, it was found by others to be practically useless. Writing on this subject in *The Field* of September 15, 1894, Lieut.-Col. Butler, of Brettenham Park, Bildeston, Suffolk, remarked:

' I strongly recommend those who have taken part in the correspondence on this subject to try the Brailsford trap, which catches all kinds of vermin alive and uninjured, and is far more effective and durable than any other trap I have yet seen. It consists of a wire cage very strongly made, and open at both ends, the doors being kept up by a simple method of setting.

There is a treadle inside, and as soon as that is touched the doors close and the victim is imprisoned. I have had many of these traps in use for some years, set in runs and at drains about my garden, where they remain the whole year round, and I scarcely ever visit them without finding something caught. For stoats, weasels, hedgehogs, rats, squirrels, rabbits, and almost every other kind of quadruped they are invaluable, and one advantage they possess over other traps is that they can be set all through the winter, as neither frost nor snow affects them. In setting them in runs under shelving banks or by the side of wire netting, I usually make wings at each end of fir boughs, or something of that kind, to guide the animal in, but when set at drains or holes, it is only necessary to make a wing at the end furthest from the hole, the trap at the other end fitting close up to the entrance of the drain. If a rabbit is found freshly killed by a stoat or weasel, it is a good plan to place it inside the trap at one end, and to set it with only one door open (the door, of course, furthest from the rabbit), so that the stoat has to step on the table to get to it. I find these traps most useful also set in this way, *i.e.* with only one door open, for catching ferrets that have laid up. In fact, if set at the main entrance of the earth the ferret is in, and the rest of the holes stopped, it is certain to be found caught in the morning, especially if a bait be used. It is as easy to set them in the dark, if visited at night, as by daylight ; and for all-round use they are, in my opinion, by far the best traps yet invented. I may add, in conclusion, that they are made in different sizes, the smallest being for mice, and from that upwards to any size ordered ; but I have found the size for cats and rabbits the best for general use.' [1]

It is very important when setting snares for rabbits to have one's hands clean—that is to say, free from any smell of powder, rabbits or dogs ; for, as already remarked, rabbits have a very keen sense of smell, and will keep clear of any trap or snare that to their perception is evidently tainted by human contact. Some keepers when trapping will advocate the use of an old pair of hedging gloves. A good plan, however, is first of all to wash one's hands well in soap and water, and then to rub them with mould scraped up near the place where the snare is to be set. When it is time to put the wire into shape, and smooth out any bends or kinks in it, this should be done, not with the bare finger and thumb, but with a bit of wash-leather between them. It is easily carried in the waistcoat pocket, and a snare rubbed down with this will be

[1] This trap may be obtained from Messrs. Artingstall & Co., manufacturers, Warrington, Lancashire.

found to run as smoothly as possible when touched by a rabbit. Moreover, this intercepts any scent from the bare hand.

Snares set in the morning, says an old keeper, catch twice as many rabbits as those set in the evening or afternoon, because the scent gets off and evaporates during the day, whereas in the evening the dews fall and preserve the scent freshly all night, thus warning off the rabbits. The same thing applies to trapping as well as snaring.

Taking rabbits in nets is a much more serious business than either trapping or snaring, and is certainly more deserving of the name of 'sport.' It may be considered under the following headings : (1) netting with the use of ferrets ; (2) with long-nets outside coverts, when large numbers are wanted for the market ; (3) gate-nets ; (4) purse-nets, and (5) drop-down-nets for keeping rabbits out while at feed, when a good show is wanted for the next day's shooting.

With regard to nets for ferreting, we have already indicated, in a previous chapter, the desirability of having some good ferrets, and have given directions for managing them and keeping them in good health. A good terrier that will 'mark' well at the entrance of a burrow is equally desirable. He must have a good nose that will enable him, on visiting one hole after another, to tell at once whether there is a rabbit 'at home' or not, and he must be absolutely mute. His business is simply to aid the warrener by pointing, or 'marking' as it is termed, at the entrance of a burrow which holds a rabbit, and thus to save a considerable amount of time and trouble.

The net used for this purpose is about 3 feet by 2 feet, the narrower sides having brass rings fastened to them, for pegging down, when necessary. It is thrown over the hole when the dog has 'marked,' a ferret is then introduced, and the rabbit is bolted into the net. It is much better to have the net slack than pegged down tight, as the rabbit is then more likely to get rolled up in it, instead of going back, as it would attempt to do, on feeling the net strained.

The performance may be varied by bolting the rabbit with a fuse instead of a ferret, on which subject we shall have more to say anon.

The 'long-net' is a useful thing in the hands of rightful owners, but its utility, unfortunately, is well known to poachers, who do not scruple to make good use of it whenever they get a chance. The employment of the 'long-net,' in fact, is one of the most troublesome forms of poaching with which game-keepers have to contend. Its extreme lightness, when made of silk, and the great lengths which may be carried without inconvenience, enable it to be readily transported from one part of the country to another, and as easily concealed.

Should there be too many rabbits in a particular covert, and comparatively few where wanted on a remote part of the shooting, the capture of a sufficient number may be easily effected with the 'long-net.' It is usually made in lengths of from 50 to 100 yards or more, and the width is generally about 5 feet, the meshes, $2\frac{1}{2}$ in. square, being large enough to allow a very small rabbit to get through. Long-nets are usually set about two yards from the side of the covert. If further away, the rabbits are more likely to see persons moving near them than if closer to the covert.

In the second series of his 'Letters to Young Shooters' (p. 419), Sir R. Payne-Gallwey writes : 'When you use nets to catch rabbits, have them made with their lower halves of light cord, and their upper of dark (this does not add to the cost), the lower and lighter half will then appear to a rabbit as an opening under the darker part, and he will un-hesitatingly run into it.' We are not told, however, how long the light-coloured cord will remain so. Not long probably ; for a few nights' work over wet grass, and a few tramplings under foot when setting or picking up, will very soon cause the net to get dirty and to look all of one colour. To work it effectively, a tolerably dark night should be selected, with the wind blowing from the covert. A number of hazel pegs are prepared about two and a half feet long, with a bit cut out of the top of each so as to form a shoulder. One man carries the pegs, another the net gathered up by coiling the top line, and putting a little strap through to buckle the folds together till wanted. The former begins by driving in a peg, and then another and another at intervals of ten paces apart; the latter follows, giving the top string of the net one turn round the top of each peg to hold it in position. This must be done as noise-lessly as possible, and when all is in readiness, one of the men, making a circuit to get round the rabbits (which on a dry night will feed a long way out from covert), gradually drives them in, while the other, with one or more helpers as the length of net may require, stays back to extricate them from the net, or to knock them on the head with a stick as they try to force their way through.

A dog that will hunt mute, and has a good turn of speed, is invaluable for this kind of work, as he can get so quickly and yet so quietly round the rabbits, and work them in the required direction as a colley works sheep. Sometimes a few hares get 'run in,' but as a rule they escape on account of their feeding at a greater distance from covert, and, being very cautious when alarmed, .they break away right or left instead of going forward, while rabbits will rush back to the place they came from as fast as their legs can carry them. Indeed, so prone are they to do this, that it is not always necessary to get right round the field before beginning to drive them, for they will commence to run home if man or dog shows up on either side of them, or even between them and the net. To save time and to ensure pushing up any rabbits that may be squatting, a long line, called by poachers 'a dead dog,' is sometimes used and is trailed across the field by a man at each end.

It may so happen that an owner of coverts may not require to use 'long-nets' on his ground, having no occasion to send any large number of rabbits away at one time. Or he may prefer to shoot them, or leave them to the tender mercies of the warrener and his ferrets. In this case it will be well to see that poachers are not allowed a chance to help themselves in this way, and a keeper or watcher should go round the coverts every night, or every other night, and run the rabbits in, taking care to see by daylight that the fields lying round it have been well 'bushed.' After being treated like this for a time, the rabbits will

learn to feed earlier in the evening, and will contrive
to get their supper before the time comes for running
them in.   They will then be out again for breakfast at
daylight, when netting them would be impracticable.

A modified form of 'long-net' is the 'gate-net'
(or 'sheet-net' as it is called in some parts of the
country) used for taking hares.   This is about six
feet wide, and six or seven yards long.   When supported on sticks it stands about a yard high, the
lower half being spread on the ground towards the
gateway in front of which it is hung.

A still smaller net, the 'purse-net,' is used for
taking hares as they come through a meuse.   It is
made something like a landing-net but longer, with a
running string through every mesh round the mouth
of it.   This kind of net is inserted in a meuse through
which a hare is expected to pass, with the opening of
course facing the covert or ground about to be driven.
Two or three of the top meshes are forced into the
interstices of the wall to keep the net up, and are
held there with pieces of short stick, or it may be
with little lumps of stiff clay, if there happens to be
any at hand.   The end of the running string is
fastened to a peg which is driven into the ground, and
all is then in readiness.   The dog does the rest, and
the hare if anywhere within reach is very soon in the

net. This is truly a poacher's contrivance, but has its legitimate use when live hares are wanted to stock ground at a distance.

The last net to be described is the 'drop-down-net.' Everyone who owns game-coverts is familiar with the fact that rabbits have a provoking habit of feeding a little way outside their burrows, where at a respectable distance they may be viewed perhaps in hundreds; but the instant an attempt is made to approach them within shooting distance, they bolt back into covert and are safe. It must often have struck others as it has the writer, that if a net could be contrived, elevated, and fixed in such a way as to drop behind the rabbits when they are fairly out, and so cut off their retreat, a much better toll might be taken of their number, and if it were thought desirable this might be effected without any shooting, and in a way which need not disturb the pheasants. A contrivance of this kind has been patented by Mr. A. R. Warren, of Warren's Court, Lisarda, Co. Cork, and has been de-scribed in *The Field* of December 3, 1892, with illustrations.

The net recommended is of 2-in. mesh, 3 ft. deep, 100 yards long, made of the finest Irish flax, with plaited running lines of the same, and may be obtained of the patentee with the apparatus, if

desired.[1]   The bottom line of the net, or that which
rests on the ground, runs freely through the meshes,
and is not made taut at intervals like the top line.
One end of the bottom line is fastened to the net,
and has a ring on it to slip over a pole which is
driven into the ground and maintained at an angle of
70° by wire stays and pegs.   The other end of the
bottom line is not fastened, and is three or four yards
longer than the net, so that it may be tightened or
slackened at will.   The top line is set in the usual
way for long nets, and should be out of reach of a
rabbit when standing up.   Intermediate poles are
then twisted into the top line so as to have it perfectly
taut from end to end.

Thus far in the mode of setting there is nothing
new ; the novelty consists in the lifting up and setting
the bottom line with triggers in such a way that upon
a pull of the trigger cord, each trigger releases the
short arm of a lever on which the bottom line rests,
and so drops it.   The mode of setting is somewhat
as follows :—To the intermediate poles are attached
the 'elevator' by means of brass sockets.   These
'elevators' have brass catches or holding pieces at
the back, into which one end of a bar or trigger is

---

[1] The London agents are Messrs. Hughes, Eli & Hughes,
76 Chancery Lane.

inserted and held, so that it may turn in a horizontal plane from either side. Below the catch there is pivoted a lever, with the long arm hanging down, the short arm up. The bottom line of the net is now hung upon the long arms throughout its length, the short arms being hitched under the triggers. On a pull of the trigger-cord at any reasonable distance, the triggers release the short arms of the levers, and the net drops, the rings on the end poles sliding down to the bottom. There are one or two further points, however, which may be noticed. The ' elevators ' are to be fixed on the poles with the brass catches at the backs thereof—that is, in the opposite direction from that in which the rabbits are driven. Then, at the bottom of each pole are what the inventor terms ' guides.' These are light slips of wood, about six feet in length, which are run on to spindles nearly flush with the ground. As the bottom line of the net hangs on the long levers, each ' guide ' is passed through the mesh next the line, spindle end first, brought under the net and slipped on the spindle. In this position the top end of each ' guide ' should rest in a slanting position against the bottom running line, close to the end of the lever. Looking at it sideways the net will be seen to hang between the ' guides ' and ' elevators.' The ' guides ' serve to keep the

L

net in an outward direction when falling, and keep the bottom line firmly to the ground at each pole. The advantages claimed for this method of netting are that it can be used by daylight; that before a drive the rabbits are not disturbed by any noise behind them; and that, owing to the instantaneous fall of the net, rabbits feeding even within a few feet of it cannot get back to covert before the net stops them.

Messrs. Denman, of Overton, Hants, have designed and patented a so-called drop-down fencing intended to answer the same purpose, but it is more expensive to erect, and, being made of wire instead of string-netting, is more likely to injure game going hard at it than is the case with the softer material.

We come now to a subject which may be appropriately dealt with in the present chapter, since it affects the question 'how to make rabbits lie out.' It will be admitted by most people who have tried it that ferreting as a preliminary to a big shoot is slow work; it unnecessarily frightens the rabbits, and many get so mutilated by the ferrets that they never come aboveground again.

A good deal will depend upon the kind of ground on which they are to be 'stopped out.' If there is no covert, or very little, and that not of the right sort, all one's efforts to induce rabbits to lie out will be in vain.

Nor will it be of much avail if the grass is thick but grazed over by cattle, or disturbed by dogs, for rabbits will then get no rest, and will be very loth to stay there. There is no covert so good as brambles, and next to that long sedgy grass. If the ground is bare, a good plan is to scatter small bunches of light thorns about the fields in the spring. Through these the grass will grow up, and while, by reason of the thorns, it will escape the mouths of cattle, it will form snug lying for rabbits.

To get the latter out into ground thus prepared, or for that matter any other ground that has sufficient covert to hold them, the easiest plan is to send some men round with spades, and let them stop every hole they can find. The second day they should take a pail of paraffin,[1] and some pegs, about 8 in. long, with a slit in the top into which is inserted a piece of folded paper. These are dipped in the oil and stuck in the ground immediately opposite the holes that have been opened. On the third day all open holes should be stopped again ; on the fourth, paraffin once more ; on the fifth, stop all holes effectually ; and on the sixth day, shoot. During this time the covert all round should be left perfectly quiet and undisturbed,

[1] Some keepers mix two-thirds paraffin with one-third animal oil.

and after the shoot all traces of paraffin should be removed.

If paraffin is not to be obtained just when wanted, spirits of tar will answer the purpose. One who has tried it recommends the use of a rope's end frayed out, soaked in paraffin, and lighted at the windward holes of the burrows.

The use of sulphur is not to be recommended, for two reasons : if only a moderate dose be applied, it will cause a rabbit not merely to bolt, but to desert the hole for ever; while if the fumes are too strong, the result will be suffocation on the spot.

Some keepers dispense with 'stopping' and content themselves with sticking the pegs in front of the holes two clear nights before the coverts are shot. Our late friend, Mr. T. J. Mann, of Hyde Hall, Sawbridgeworth, one of the most practical sportsmen that ever lived, had another plan which he found to be very effectual, and he thus described it for the benefit of readers of *The Field.* 'Two days before we shoot the woods,' he said, 'the keepers take a lined ferret on the back of which is smeared a strong solution of asafœtida. The ferret is then worked a short way into all the holes which can be got at. The good sport subsequently obtained in the rough meadows round the woods affords the best criterion as to the success of this plan '—and from personal experience we can vouch for its efficacy. The only drawback is the time it takes when a large number of burrows have to be worked.

One other method of bolting rabbits remains to be noticed, namely by means of a fuse. Several different kinds have been advocated ; perhaps the most efficient, judging by results, are those made by Messrs. Brunton & Co., Cambrian Safety Fuse Works, Wrexham. It is on record that in the park at Weald Hall, Brentwood, Essex, after the use of some of these fuses a party of six guns shot 1,027 rabbits in one day, and on the following day over the same beat 405 more.[1]

It is to be observed, however, that in the employment of fuses, success must in some measure depend upon the nature of the ground ; for where the burrows are large and rambling, it has been found by experience that fuses are of little or no use.[2]

[1] *The Field*, November 12 and 26, 1892.
[2] *Ibid.* February 4 and 11, 1893.

CHAPTER VI

POACHING

IN the last chapter we described the legitimate
employment of traps, snares, and nets for the purpose of killing or taking rabbits.   It is the illegitimate
use of these (*inter alia*) that constitutes poaching.

It was correctly observed by the late Richard
Jefferies that there are three kinds of poachers : the
local men ; the raiders coming in gangs from a distance ; and the 'mouchers'—fellows who do not
make precisely a profession of it, but who occasionally
loiter along the roads and hedges, picking up whatever they can lay hands on.   Of the three, perhaps,
the largest amount of business is done by the local
men, who are often sober and apparently industrious
individuals working during the day at some handi-
craft in the village.   Their great object is to avoid
suspicion, knowing that success will be proportionate
to their skill in cloaking their operations ; for in a
small community when a man is suspected, it is

comparatively easy to watch him, and a poacher knows that, if he is watched, he must sooner or later be caught. Secrecy is not so very difficult; for it is only with certain classes that he need practise concealment; his own class will hold their peace.

Perhaps the most promising position for a man who makes a science of it, says the observant writer just quoted, is a village at the end of a range of downs, generally fringed with large woods on the lower slopes. He has then ground to work alternately, according to the character of the weather and the changes of the moon. If the weather be wet, windy, or dark from the absence of the moon, then the wide open hills are safe; while, on the other hand, the woods are practically inaccessible, for a man must have the eyes of a cat to see to do his work in the impenetrable blackness of the plantations. So that upon a bright night the judicious poacher prefers the woods, because he can see his way, and avoids the hills, because, having no fences to speak of, a watcher may detect him a mile off.

Meadows with high banks and thick hedges may be worked almost at any time, for one side of the hedge is sure to cast a shadow, and instant cover is afforded by the bushes and ditches. Such meadows are the happy hunting-grounds of the local poacher for that reason, especially if not far distant from woods and consequently overrun with rabbits.

Rabbits are not easily dislodged in rain, for they avoid getting wet as much as possible ; they bolt best when it is dry and still. Nor will a poacher who means ferreting choose a windy night (though it is otherwise when he is after pheasants), for he has to depend a great deal on his sense of hearing to know when a rabbit is moving in the 'bury,' and where it is likely to bolt, so as to lay hold of it the moment it is in the net.

Poachers who use ferrets prefer white ones for night work, as they are more easily seen, and are not so likely to be picked up by a dog in mistake for a rabbit, although poachers' dogs as a rule are generally too well trained to make such mistakes. Keepers are only too glad to get hold of poachers' ferrets when they can, for they are almost certain to be good ones.

The favourite implement, however, with rabbit poachers is, no doubt, the wire snare. This is easily carried about in the pocket, to be set as occasion or opportunity may arise, and is easily removed.[1] It is otherwise with nets, which usually require the

[1] Several instances have been reported in which two rabbits have been caught in one snare, either by the legs, or one by the leg the other by the neck. See *The Field*, April 2 and 7, 1892, and January 30, 1897.

attention of more than one person, thus increasing the chance of detection. The keeper, who in the course of his rounds may happen to detect a number of 'wires,' has two courses open to him. He may either pull up the pegs and take the snares bodily away (unless, of course, they have been set by an 'occupier' on land in his occupation, when the keeper has no right to remove them [1]), or he may watch the place to discover who comes to look at them. In the latter case he should give the culprit time, and if possible catch him in the act of taking a rabbit out of a snare. The plan of putting a dead rabbit in a wire and allowing the poacher to find it is not to be recommended, for in the event of a prosecution this would afford a loophole for escape, since the keeper, if cross-examined for the defence, would have to admit that he himself placed the rabbit where it was found. It is much better to allow the culprit to walk away with any rabbit he may have seen him kill, and then to question him.

In the case of 'long-netting' it is better to counteract the setting by 'bushing' the field, or driving the rabbits into cover at night (about 10 P.M. and again about 1 A.M.) with a good dog, than to take proceedings against the offenders after the rabbits have been killed and removed.

[1] See Hobbs *v.* Symons, *The Field*, March 31, 1888.

Some keepers advocate turning out a few white rabbits, which are more readily seen at night than the others, and by keeping a watch on them observe whether they disappear. This will show whether there is any poaching going on or not; though a wily poacher who knows his business will, of course, take care to let any white ones go that he may happen to capture. The most effectual way, however, to prevent 'long-netting' is to bush the fields around the coverts, not with fixed bushes or stakes, but with loose thorns, or short pieces of bramble or furze strewn loosely about in the field. These will be dragged by the net and cause it to become so hampered and entangled as to be useless. A gamekeeper, writing in *The Field* of August 4, 1894, recommended the scattering of small pieces of wire netting,[1] but although this might defeat the poachers, it would hardly suit farmers who have sheep or other stock to turn on the land.

When coverts are surrounded by stone walls, it is usual to leave openings called ' meuses ' here and there for the hares and rabbits to go in and out. A poacher who intends to use a 'purse-net' will previously block up all the 'meuses' except those in which he intends to hang his nets, and, to enable him to distinguish at

[1] This was also recommended by another correspondent, *The Field*, January 25, 1896.

night those which are blocked from those which are open, will place on the wall immediately above the open ones a loose stone, a stick, or a piece of turf to mark them. A keeper on going his rounds, therefore, should be on the look out for such objects, and when found should carefully shift them over the closed holes, and so defeat the object in view. To counteract the use of 'gate-nets,' it is not a bad plan for a keeper to use some himself for a few nights, and after catching several hares liberate them immediately. This will cause the hares to fight shy of gates, and quit the fields in some other way. Another effective plan is to paint the lower bars of the gates white, and the hares will then avoid them.

The raiders who come in gangs armed with guns and shoot the best coverts, generally selecting pheasants at roost, are usually colliers, miners, or the scum of manufacturing towns, led by some ruffian who has a knowledge of the ground. These gangs display no skill, but rely on their numbers, arms, and known desperation of character to save them from arrest, as unfortunately it very often does.

The 'mouchers' who sneak about the roads and hedgerows with dogs on Sundays, and snap up a rabbit or a hare, do not do so much damage except in the neighbourhood of large towns, where they are more numerous. Shepherds, too, sometimes require looking after, for they often have dogs which, though supposed to be used only for sheep, are extremely clever in helping their owners to get hold of a hare or rabbit. Even a ploughman will leave his horses to set a wire in a gateway or gap where he has noticed the track of a hare; but this is generally for his own eating, and is not of much consequence in comparison with the work of the real local professional. These regular hands form a class, now more numerous than ever; for the price obtainable for game from local dealers causes many a man to turn poacher in a small way who would otherwise lead a respectable and honest life. Moreover, the spread of railways into the most outlying districts enables poachers, or their aiders and abettors, to get hampers of game speedily out of reach of the local policeman.

The people who require most looking after, however, are the small higglers, or 'general dealers' as they call themselves, who go round the countryside with a cart, and, under pretence of selling fish, or buying and selling poultry, are frequently in league with poachers, especially during the egging season, when they become possessed of large quantities of pheasants' and partridges' eggs. As an instance of the mischief which may be done by these gentry, it may

AN OLD HAND

be noted that on May 26, 1898, one Charles Gooch, a marine-store dealer, was prosecuted by the Field Sports Protection Association, at the Saxmundham Petty Sessions, where, being convicted of being in unlawful possession of 655 partridges' eggs, he was fined one shilling per egg, or 32*l.* 15*s.* and costs, or in default two months' imprisonment with hard labour. It would be well if this example were followed more frequently by justices at petty sessions in other parts of the country, and much might be done to prevent poaching if County Councillors and Boards of Guardians would follow the lead of those at Wimborne who, on July 30, 1898, refused to grant to a general dealer a licence to deal in game.[1]

The power to grant such licences has been transferred from the Justices to the Guardians, and the Act conferring such power (1 & 2 Will. IV. cap. 32) expressly provides (Sect. 18) that 'a licence to deal in game *cannot be granted* to an innkeeper or licensed victualler, or person licensed to sell beer by retail, or to the owner, guard, or driver of any mail coach or conveyance used for carrying the mails, or of any stage coach, waggon, van, or other public conveyance, *or to a carrier or higgler*, or to a person in the employment of any of the above.'

[1] For report of this case see *The Field*, August 6, 1898, p. 267.

To judge by the local press reports of the poaching cases which come before the magistrates at petty sessions, it would seem that the majority of convictions are for poaching rabbits, the proceedings being taken under the principal Game Act, 1831 (1 & 2 Will. IV. cap. 32), the Night Poachers' Act, 1828 (9 Geo. IV. cap. 69) modified by the Night Poaching Act, 1844 (7 & 8 Vict. cap. 29), the Larceny Act, 1861 (24 & 25 Vict. cap. 96), or the Poaching Prevention Act, 1862 (25 & 26 Vict. cap. 114).

As a good deal of ignorance prevails on the subject of the law relating to rabbits, not only amongst gamekeepers, who can hardly be supposed to know very much about it, but also amongst their employers, who might be expected to be better informed, it may not be out of place in a volume pertaining exclusively to 'The Rabbit' to devote a few pages to the consideration of cases which continually arise, and to the law which governs them. A little plain law on the subject may be acceptable both to masters and servants, and we shall endeavour so to expound it as to free it as much as possible from technicalities, confining attention chiefly to the duties of gamekeepers (in respect of rabbits) as regulated by Acts of Parliament.

Perhaps the simplest mode of dealing with the subject will be to look into the provisions of the above-mentioned statutes, and see how they affect the questions which are likely to arise where rabbits are concerned.

With regard to trespass *by day* in pursuit of game or rabbits (coneys they are styled in the Statute) Section 30 of the principal Game Act (1 & 2 Will. IV. cap. 32) expressly states that if any person shall commit a trespass by entering in the day-time [1] upon any land in search or pursuit of game *or coneys*, he shall be liable on conviction to a penalty not exceeding 2*l.* and costs, or, in default, to imprisonment with hard labour for a term not exceeding two months. And if the offence be committed by a party of five or more persons, the penalty on conviction may be 5*l.* and costs, or, in default, imprisonment with hard labour as before.

In such case anyone may lay an information, and one justice may receive it. It need not be in writing, though it usually is, and it need not be on oath, unless a warrant for the apprehension of an offender be applied for by the informant, and then the information must be a sworn one. It must be for one offence

[1] Section 34 of this Act states that *day-time* shall be deemed to commence at the beginning of the last hour before sunrise, and to conclude at the expiration of the first hour after sunset. Night will therefore mean the remaining portion of the twenty-four hours.

on one day only, but an information against several
persons for a joint offence will hold good.   In any
case the prosecution must be originated within
three calendar months after the commission of the
offence.

If an offender, after being served with a summons,
does not appear, the keeper (or other informant) may
either apply for a warrant or proceed in his absence.

We need not here concern ourselves with the
defence likely to be set up by a rabbit poacher, for
that is a matter to be determined by the justices at the
hearing of the summons ; unless a *bona-fide* claim of
right is pleaded, in which case the magistrates' jurisdiction would be ousted, and the dispute would have to
be settled in a superior court.   But cases may arise in
which, for want of proper instruction, a keeper may
be induced to let an offender escape.   For example,
it is settled law that a right of common carries with it
no right to kill the ground game on a common which
belongs to the lord of the manor.[1]   If, therefore, a
gamekeeper of the latter sees a person shooting
rabbits on a common, and on remonstrating with
him is informed that he is a commoner and merely
exercising his privilege, he should reply civilly that he

---

[1] *Watkins* v. *Major*, 44 L.J. M.C. 164 and L.R. 10 C.P.
662.

is mistaken ; that commoners have no right to kill rabbits ; that he must desist ; and that if he continues to shoot, he will be summoned. The owner of a free warren, also, may prosecute tenants of land within the limits of the free warren if they kill rabbits, or give permission to others to do so ; and he should instruct his keeper to let it be known that he claims the rabbits on the land of such persons under a grant of free warren (see p. 55). It has been decided also in several reported cases that a dog found hunting rabbits in a warren may be killed by the keeper or warrener ; and the owner of a franchise of a park may kill a dog chasing game in the park.[1] In other cases, a keeper would do well to abstain from shooting a trespassing dog, or he may find himself made liable in damages to the owner.[2] His proper course is to give the owner of the dog notice in writing to restrain him from trespassing, and to intimate that, unless he does so, traps will be set.

Should any doubt arise in the mind of a gamekeeper as to the ownership of a hedge in which he may find snares set for rabbits or hares, he may note

[1] Vere *v.* Lord Cawdor, 11 East, 568 ; Protheroe *v.* Matthews, 5 C. and P. 581.

[2] See the report of a case at Cardiff in which a gamekeeper was ordered to pay 12*l.* for shooting a dog while in pursuit of a rabbit. — *The Field*, February 27, 1897.

M

that a hedge is always presumed to belong to the person in whose field the ditch is *not* ; the reason being that the person who makes a hedge bank by cutting a ditch must throw up the soil on his own land, and not on his neighbour's ; he thus becomes the owner of the hedge. If there are two ditches, one on each side of a hedge, the ownership of the hedge will depend on the past exercise of rights over it, or the liability to repair it.

It often happens that a poacher, with a view to avoid a charge of trespass, confines his operations to one side or the other of a high road, along which he may pretend to be walking quietly if disturbed. It is well to remember, therefore, that a highway (subject to the right of the public to use it for all usual and lawful purposes) is deemed to be land in the possession of adjoining owners and occupiers, and therefore a poacher under such circumstances may be treated as if he were a trespasser on the adjoining land. Moreover, if he is using a gun for shooting through the hedge, he may not only be prosecuted for trespass in pursuit of game, but may be summoned under Section 72 of the Highway Act (5 & 6 Will. IV. cap. 50) for discharging a gun within fifty feet from the centre of the highway. By shooting from a high road a trespass is committed as if the shooter had entered the adjacent field. This was decided by the Court of Queen's Bench in the case of Regina *v.* Pratt, 24 L J. (N.S.) 113. If the facts warrant it, he may also be prosecuted for shooting game without a licence.

It is a question for the justices to determine whether a defendant is 'in pursuit of game' or not. In a case tried at Cheltenham in January, 1892, in which two persons were summoned for trespass in pursuit of game, it was contended on their behalf that, although they had a dog and gun, there was no evidence of their being 'in pursuit of game.' The magistrates, however, considered that their intention was sufficiently evident, and fined them ten shillings each and costs.

If the owner of a hedge which he proposes to ferret, steps over into his neighbour's field for the purpose of shooting any rabbits that may be put out to him, he is clearly a trespasser, for it is only by permission that a person can stand on his neighbour's land for the purpose of killing game started on his own property.

Should it happen that a person convicted of trespassing in pursuit of game, or rabbits, under Section 30 of the Act 1 & 2 Will. IV. cap. 32, is the holder of a gun or game licence, that licence will become forfeited, and if he intends to shoot again, he will have to take out a fresh licence under penalties prescribed in the Game Licence Act, 1860, and the Gun Licence Act, 1870. A gamekeeper, therefore, who has obtained a conviction will do well to bear this fact in mind.

Disputes often arise as to who has or who has not the right to kill rabbits, and as the law which formerly held good has been materially altered by the Ground Game Act, passed in 1880, the consideration of this part of the subject may be reserved for another chapter, in which we propose to deal exclusively with the provisions of that particular statute. Since that Act, however, does not affect the rights of owners and occupiers under leases executed before the passing of the Act, it may be well to note here that rabbits do not come within the definition of 'game' laid down in the principal Game Act, and therefore, where 'game' only is reserved to a landlord *under a lease dated prior to* 1880, the tenant may kill the rabbits or authorise his servants to kill them for him,[1] but *not* strangers; for the game being reserved, the permission of the tenant is no defence to strangers prosecuted

[1] Spicer *v.* Barnard, 28 L.J. M.C. 176; and Padwick *v.* King, 29 L.J. M.C. 42. It is otherwise in the case of tenancies created since the passing of the Ground Game Act, as will be explained in the next chapter.

by the landlord for trespassing in pursuit of it, or of
woodcocks, snipes, quails, landrails, or rabbits.[1]

Two very important points remain to be considered,
the right to arrest, and the right to search. As probably more mistakes are made by keepers in these
matters than in any others with which they have to
deal, it will be well to state clearly how the law
stands.

Any person may order an ordinary trespasser to
quit his land, and may remove him if he refuses to
do so, but he has no power at common law to sum-
marily arrest him. If, however, the offender be
trespassing in search of game, Section 31 of the
principal Game Act authorises any person having the
right of killing the game, or the occupier of the land,
or the gamekeeper or servant of either of them, to
arrest him under certain specified circumstances ;
namely, if he refuses to tell his real name or place of
abode, or gives a false name and address (to the
keeper's knowledge), or wilfully continues on the land
or returns to it, he may be apprehended and taken
as soon as possible before a Justice of the Peace,[2]

---

[1] Pryce *v.* Davies, 35 J.P. 374 ; and Morden *v.* Porter,
29 L.J. M.C. 213.

[2] The section requires that he must not be detained more
than twelve hours, and if, for any sufficient reason, he cannot
be brought before a Justice of the Peace within that time, he

and on being convicted of any such offence, is liable to a penalty not exceeding 5*l.* and costs, or in default, two months' imprisonment with hard labour.

If any of the parties authorised as above can see game in possession of the trespasser, they may demand it, and if refused, may seize it, but they may not search a person on suspicion, nor can they seize his gun. The only person empowered to search is a constable under circumstances mentioned in the Poaching Prevention Act, 1862, to be presently referred to.

Under the Night Poachers' Act, 1828 (9 Geo. IV. cap. 69) modified by the Night Poaching Act, 1844 (7 & 8 Vict. cap. 29) any one taking or killing game or rabbits *at night*,[1] either on open or enclosed land, or upon any highway or the sides thereof, or entering such places for the purpose, is liable on conviction to three months' imprisonment with hard labour for a first offence, six months' for a second offence, and a still longer term for any subsequent offence.[2] Such person also may be apprehended,

must be discharged, and proceeded against by summons or warrant, as if no such apprehension had taken place.

[1] Night is deemed to commence at the expiration of the first hour after sunset and to conclude at the beginning of the last hour before sunrise. See p. 159, note.

[2] It is important to bear in mind that before he can be convicted he must have actually killed or taken a rabbit. It is

and delivered over to a constable, to be brought before two Justices of the Peace to be dealt with as the Act provides. If such person offers violent resistance, and assaults those authorised to apprehend him, he is guilty of a misdemeanour, and is liable on conviction to transportation for seven years, or to imprisonment with hard labour for two years.

The Larceny Act, 1861 (Section 17) makes it an offence to kill hares and rabbits *at night* ' in a warren ' (see p. 57), an extension, as it were, of the Night Poaching Acts which relate to taking or killing game or rabbits ' in open or enclosed lands.' Whether the land in question is ' a warren,' or not, may be a question for the determination of the justices.[1] If it be quite certain that the offence was committed ' in a warren,' the offender may be prosecuted under the Larceny Act, otherwise under the Night Poaching Acts. One must, of course, bear in mind the distinction between an ordinary warren and the right of free warren, as explained in a former chapter (see p. 52).

not sufficient for him to be merely on the land in search of rabbits. The keeper therefore, if he sees a trespasser at night whom he has reason to suspect, should give him time before making his appearance. The reason for this anomaly, which arises on a question of construction of the Act, is fully explained in an article on ' Rabbit Poaching by Night,' in *The Field* of February 15, 1890.

[1] Bevan *v.* Hopkinson, 34 L.T. 142. See p. 58, note.

Poachers will sometimes capture in one night with the long net more rabbits than they can carry away. They will accordingly be compelled to hide them, and remove them subsequently as best they may. If they escape detection when capturing them, but are caught while removing them, the rabbits being then dead, it becomes a question whether the offence is one of larceny or not. The point was decided in the case of Regina *v.* Lewis Townley, reported in *The Field* of April 29, 1871. A poacher, who had assisted in taking 126 rabbits which were concealed with 400 yards of netting, was subsequently caught removing them, and was prosecuted and convicted of larceny for stealing them. But on appeal, the Court for the Consideration of Crown Cases Reserved quashed the conviction on the ground that the act of killing and removing was continuous, and that that which was not larceny in its inception could not be so in its natural fulfilment of the original intention.

On the other hand, if the offender had been charged with poaching and convicted, the conviction would probably have been affirmed. This is shown by the case of Horn *v.* Raine.[1] In this case, the poacher Raine, standing in his own allotment, fired over the wall at a grouse that was sitting on Lord Westbury's

[1] *Law Times*, July 16, 1898.

land adjoining, and killed it. He did not at once seek to remove it, and Horn (Lord Westbury's game-keeper), who was attracted by the shot, found the dead bird and removed it without being seen by Raine. Some hours later Raine returned, and climbed over the wall and began looking for the dead bird. He was charged with trespassing on the land in pursuit of game. The magistrates dismissed the charge on the ground that the distance of time between the act of killing and the act of taking prevented them from treating the two as one continuous act. A Divisional Court, however, on a case stated, remitted the case to the magistrates with directions to convict on the ground that on the facts stated the killing and taking constituted one continuous act.

We come now to the Poaching Prevention Act, 1862 (25 & 26 Vict. cap. 114), the provisions of which apply to rabbits as well as to game. It is an extremely important Act, because it empowers police constables in certain cases to search suspected persons without a warrant, a proceeding which, as we have seen (p. 165), is not in the power of any owner, occupier, gamekeeper or other person acting under his or their directions.

Section 2 of this Act enables a constable to search, in any highway, street, or public place, any person

suspected of coming from land where he has been unlawfully in pursuit of game, and to take from him
any game, eggs of game, *or rabbits* that may be found
in his possession, or any gun, part of gun, or nets,
or engines used for killing or taking game. It also
enables a constable to stop and search any cart, or
conveyance, in which he suspects any of these things
to be concealed, and, if found, to seize and detain
them. In such a case, the constable must apply to
a magistrate for a summons citing the offender to
appear before two justices at petty sessions, if in
England or Ireland, or before a sheriff or any two
justices if in Scotland, to be dealt with as the Act
provides.

This statute, in the words of Mr. Justice Byles,[1]
' not only creates a new criminal jurisdiction, but
changes the burden of proof in a criminal case, and
therefore we must give it a strict construction. Now it
appears that there are four requisites : *first*, that the
suspected person should be found on the highway, &c. ;
secondly, that there should be good ground of suspicion
that he has come from land where he has been unlawfully pursuing game, and that he has in his possession game unlawfully obtained, or certain other
specified articles ; *thirdly*, that he should have in his

---

[1] Clarke *v.* Crowder and others, L.R. 4 C.P. 638.

possession on the highway such game, &c. ; *fourthly*, that game, &c. should there be *found* on him, *i.e.* seen, or heard, or felt on him, so as to constitute a finding by the senses of a witness.'

As pointed out by Mr. Warry, one of the latest writers on the game laws,[1] this is the only statute which directly invokes the aid of the police for the protection of game. A constable is authorised under Sections 9, 10 of the Gun Licence Act, 1870, to demand the production of gun licences, and may be asked to assist keepers to effect an arrest under the Game Act, 1831 (Section 31), or the Night Poaching Act, 1828 (Section 2), but the public have generally viewed with disfavour the employment of constables to assist in the preservation of game. In consequence, however, of frequent breaches of the peace and murderous assaults arising from the necessity of arresting poachers, this statute was passed to assist keepers in this respect, that (whether from information received from them or otherwise) a constable on duty might be enabled to stop and search persons on their return from what he might suspect to be a poaching expedition, and if game was found on them, to lay the same onus on such persons of accounting

---

[1] *The Game Laws of England, with an Appendix of the Statutes relating to Game.* London, Stevens & Sons, 1896.

for the possession of it, as the law lays upon the possession of stolen property.

It is not to be expected, nor would it be possible in the limited space here at disposal, that we should enter into more minute details of the law concerning rabbits, or consider its application in every case that might be likely to arise. All that we have attempted to do in these pages is to give a few broad outlines for the guidance of those masters and servants who, having rabbits to care for and protect from poachers, may desire to know briefly what are their legal rights and remedies.

It remains to consider the provisions of the Ground Game Act, which is of such importance to owners, occupiers, and shooting tenants as to require separate treatment in another chapter.

CHAPTER VII

THE GROUND GAME ACT

IT may be said without much fear of contradiction that no Act of Parliament in modern times has caused more misunderstanding, ill-feeling and general dissatisfaction than the Ground Game Act of 1880. It has pleased nobody, except perhaps the promoters of it. Naturally it has not pleased the landlord, for, regardless of the legal maxim *cujus est solum ejus est usque ad cœlum*, it has deprived him of the liberty of contract, and the right of doing what he pleases with his own. It has decreed that from the date of the passing of the Act his interest in hares and rabbits shall be shared with his tenants, who are to have as much right to kill or take them as he has himself. If he does not shoot, or preserve game for his friends to shoot, this might not at first sight appear to be of much consequence ; but if he lets his shooting it makes all the difference in the world—a difference, that is to say, in the value of the shooting, or the amount of rent which he is able to secure for it. For no shooting tenant now-a-days will give as much rent as he would be willing to pay if the landlord could let him the exclusive right to kill hares and rabbits, which under the new *régime* he is unable to do, unless he happens to be an owner in occupation of his own land.

Shooting tenants with some reason complain that things are very much altered for the worse. They find that the tenants, or 'occupiers' as they are termed in the Act, under cover of exercising their privileges and keeping down the ground game, are perpetually disturbing the ground at all seasons of the year. Whether the partridges or pheasants are sitting or have led off their broods makes no difference to them. They are trapping, wiring, or shooting all the year round, and the evidence adduced on the hearing of summonses for trespass in pursuit of game shows only too plainly that they are not always careful to confine their attention to fur, but kill winged game when they think they can do so without risk of detection. The result of this constant disturbance of the ground, especially during the egging season, is only too apparent when the first of September comes round. The frequent ferreting of the hedgerows causes many a partridge to desert the eggs, and those which contrive to hatch off often become so wild as to be almost unapproachable. Hares there are none, or so few in comparison to what there were, that the shooting tenant is woefully disappointed. Nor can rabbits be found in anything like their accustomed number. On many farms, excepting those which adjoin large coverts not included in the letting to the tenant farmer, rabbits are almost cleared off; and every shooting man knows how coneys tell up in the bag at the end of a day's shooting. It is not the loss of their intrinsic value that is deplored, but the loss of sport which is implied by their absence.

Nor are the tenant farmers much better pleased than the landlords with the result of the new legislation, although the Act was passed ostensibly in their interest—'to protect their crops from injury and loss by ground game.' Formerly if a standing crop was damaged by the depredations of hares and rabbits, the farmer made a claim against the landlord, a valuer was appointed to look into the matter, and an amount of compensation was agreed upon which was generally deducted from the rent. In some cases a landlord who had paid, or allowed, compensation for some years on this score would perhaps lose patience, and in order to relieve himself for the future of this annual claim, would consent to reduce the rent at once by an agreed amount for the remainder of the term, on condition that he should hear no more of compensation for damage done by ground game. This satisfied both parties. At all events the landlord had the right to make his own terms in regard to the letting of his own land (which under the Ground Game Act he is now precluded from doing), and the tenant had the satisfaction of knowing that he had secured perhaps a substantial reduction of rent for the remainder of his term. Now the tenant or 'occupier' has a concurrent right to the ground game, of which he cannot divest himself much as he might like to sell the exclusive right of killing it ; for any agreement in contravention of this is declared by the third section of the Act, as will be seen later, to be void. Still he is not happy, and notwithstanding that when rabbits attack his crops he has the remedy in his own hands and is at liberty to destroy them, he still seeks to get compensation when he can from the landlord, or from the tenant to whom his landlord has let the shooting over his farm. From the reported decisions in actions of this class, it would seem that, wherever a tenant in the occupancy of a farm has a right to kill rabbits, he has no claim for damage done by them to his crops, provided they are bred or burrow on his farm ; for if they are thus permitted to increase, the fault is his own. But, if his crops are damaged by rabbits reared and allowed to increase in plantations or coverts within and around the farm and which are not in his occupation, he certainly has a claim of damages (for the loss sustained) against his landlord. In the Scotch case of Inglis *v.* Moir's Tutors and Gunnis, where a tenant brought an action against both landlord and shooting tenant for damage done to crops by rabbits, it was held that the landlord was liable, but not the shooting tenant, Lord Justice Clerk in giving judgment said : ' As regards the case against the game tenant, if he did any personal act to the injury of the agricultural tenant (such as treading down corn or breaking fences) he would be responsible. But he is under no obligation to kill rabbits for the benefit of the farmer. There is no mutual obligation between them. Neither the omission to kill rabbits, nor the destruction of vermin, which are matters entirely within the power of the game tenant to do or omit, can give the agricultural tenant any just cause of action. His claim lies against his landlord under the contract with him, which is neither enlarged nor restricted by the rights given to the tenant of the shooting.' [1]

[1] See reports of claims for damage done by rabbits, Cameron *v.* Drummond, *The Field*, February 4, 1888, and Smith *v.* Brand, *The Field*, November 9, 1895.

N

Sometimes a shooting tenant is induced to consent to a clause in the lease to indemnify his landlord against claims by tenants for damage done by ground game— a proviso which should be refused unless he is very anxious to secure the shooting, and the landlord will not let it otherwise, regarding such clause as tantamount to a guarantee that the ground game will be well kept down. This happened in the case of Rashleigh and another *v.* Veale, which came before his Honour Judge Grainger in the St. Austell County Court in January, 1895, the result being that the defendant (who was the sporting tenant), as was to be expected, was held liable on his covenant.

Another grievance on the part of an 'occupier' who holds land over which someone else has a grant of 'free warren,' is that he cannot kill any rabbits at all, notwithstanding his supposed rights under the Ground Game Act. Witness the case of Lord Carnarvon *v.* Clarkson, to which allusion has been already made.[1]

There is still another class of persons who profess themselves aggrieved by the operation of the Ground Game Act—namely, the agricultural labourers. The

[1] See pp. 55, 56, and a *précis* of the case in *The Field* of May 18, 1895, under the heading 'Occupiers who have no Right to Ground Game.'

nature of the grievance may be best exemplified by
relating a conversation which the writer had some
years ago with a south-country 'beater' well known
to him.

'Well, John, how do you like the new Ground
Game Act?'

'Not at all, sur; never get a robbut now, let be
howtle.'[1]

'Oh! how's that then?'

'Why, you see, sur, when Mister C. wur head-
keeper[2] if I'd a mind to a robbut of a Saturday for
my Sunday's dinner, why, I used to go up to hisn[3] and
ask for un, aye, and get un too. Now if I goes up to
the noo keeper and asks, he ses, "Let's see," he ses,
"who do you work for?" and I ses Varmer Rye, I ses.
Well, he ses, "Then you'd better go and ask he for un;
for he have the right to kill un same as me." So I
goes to Varmer Rye and asks he, and what d'ye
think he ses; why, he ses, "I aint got no robbuts for
no one; I ca-a-nt get enough for mysel'." So I comes
away wi'out un. That's how it be, sur.'

'Well, John, what do you do now, then?'

'Do, sur? Why' (scratching his head) 'I'se forced
to help mysel', I s'pose.'

---

[1] A provincialism; 'let it be how it will.'
[2] Before the passing of the Act.
[3] Meaning 'to his house.'

Which being interpreted means, that a good honest labourer with a wife and family to support, and with perhaps only eighteen shillings a week to do it with, out of which four or five shillings a week has to go for cottage rent, turns poacher, and sooner or later is discovered by the keeper taking a rabbit out of a wire, with the usual result. And so it is that owners, occupiers, shooting tenants and agricultural labourers, all have something to say against the Act.[1]

It would not be possible within the limits of a single chapter to examine critically all the points which are suggested by a careful perusal of the Act, nor is it to be expected that we should take cognisance of the many legal technicalities which have been argued in the numerous actions at law to which this particular statute has given rise. All that we can attempt to do here is to take a general view of the object and provisions of the Ground Game Act, and point out, as briefly as possible, some of the more important legal decisions which now materially affect its bearing. The importance of this at the present time will be apparent to those who already know how the construction of particular sections by

---

[1] See the numerous letters expressive of dissatisfaction for reasons stated which appeared in *The Field* during the months of November and December 1889.

magistrates at petty sessions has been overruled by Courts of Appeal, while the utility of such a commentary as we propose to offer will, it is hoped, be acceptable to those readers who may perchance have a copy of the Act at hand, but no notes of the important cases to which we shall refer.

The full title of this Statute is ' An Act for the better protection of Occupiers of Land against injury to their Crops from Ground Game,' and it received the royal assent on September 7, 1880.

The object of the Act is not, as some persons imagine, to transfer the right to kill hares and rabbits from ' owner ' to ' occupier,' but to protect the crops from injury by ground game, and this object is equally attained whether the animals are killed by either party. It is also a mistake to suppose that the Ground Game Act gives the landlord anything. It gives him no privilege nor concurrent right. It gives the tenant the concurrent right to hares and rabbits where they are reserved. As at common law, in the absence of any agreement between landlord and tenant with regard to ground game, hares and rabbits are the property of the tenant *as occupier of the soil*, it is necessary in making agreements with tenants, that hares and rabbits should be mentioned and reserved, otherwise the landlord will have no right to kill them.

The Act contains eleven sections.

The first section provides that :

Every occupier of land shall have a right inseparable from his occupation to kill ground game thereon, concurrently with any other person who may be entitled to it, subject to the following limitations :

Subsection 1. The occupier shall kill and take ground game only by himself or by persons duly authorised by him *in writing* :

(*a*) The occupier himself and one other person authorised in writing by such occupier shall be the only persons entitled under this Act to kill ground game *with firearms* ;

(*b*) No person shall be authorised by the occupier to kill or take ground game, except members of his household resident on the land, persons in his ordinary service on such land, and one other person *bonâ fide* employed by him for reward in taking ground game.

(*c*) Every person so authorised by the occupier, on demand by any person having a concurrent right to the ground game (or any person authorised by him in writing to make such demand) shall produce his authority, and in default shall be deemed to be not an authorised person.

The term 'occupier' is not defined by the Act, but may be taken to mean the person for the time being lawfully entitled to and exercising the exclusive possession of land.   Certain persons are expressly declared *not* to be occupiers (Sect. 1, subsect. 2) ; for example, 'a person having merely a right of common,' and 'a person occupying land for grazing purposes for a period not exceeding nine months.'   These exceptions will be considered further on.

A landlord in occupation of his own land has been decided to be *not* an occupier within the meaning of the Act.[1]   But an outgoing tenant who 'holds over' for the purpose of getting in his crops has been held to be an occupier, so as to maintain or resist an action for trespass.[2]   So also persons permitted by the tenant to use small pieces of ground for the purpose of growing potatoes have been held to be 'occupiers.'[3]   When a tenant sublets his land, he ceases to be an occupier for the purposes of the Ground Game Act.

Whether the purchaser of a standing crop from an outgoing tenant having a right to be on the land for

---

[1] Smith *v.* Hunt, 54 *Law Times Reports*, 422.   This case will be considered further on when we come to discuss the right of an owner to set spring traps aboveground.   See p. 203.

[2] Boraston *v.* Green, 16 East 71 ; and Griffiths *v.* Puleston, 13 M. & W. 358.

[3] Greenslade *v.* Tapscott, 3 L. J. Ex. 328.

the purpose of removing his crop is an ‘occupier’ within the meaning of the Act, and entitled to kill ground game on the land whereon the crop is standing, is a question which has not been decided. It might well have been raised in the case of Lunt *v.* Hill, in the Nantwich County Court in January, 1895, but the only issue tried was whether an assault had been committed by the defendant in attempting to take from the plaintiff, the purchaser of the way-going crop, the rabbits which he had shot without any authority in writing from the tenant, and without a gun licence.[1]

The term ‘occupier’ will include joint tenants ; their powers of appointment of persons to kill or take ground game could only be jointly exercised ; but whether (as is probably the case) each could exercise the rights of an occupier in killing ground game by himself is a point which, so far as we are aware, has not been judicially determined.

Before proceeding to subsection 2 of the first section, it may be well to emphasise the fact that the authority given by an ‘occupier’ to kill rabbits must be *in writing.* In a case decided at Carlisle in October, 1891 (Carter Wood *v.* Rule & Rule) a shooting tenant summoned two game-dealers for unlawfully killing rabbits at night. They pleaded authority. The occu-

---

[1] See a report of the case in *The Field* of January 26, 1895.

pier, a farmer named Dunne, admitted authorising one
of them, but stated that he paid no wages or commission for the killing ; on the contrary, they paid him
something for the privilege, and they got the rabbits
for their own benefit. No authority *in writing* being
produced, the magistrates convicted.[1] The defendants,
thinking it important to obtain a legal decision whether
or not a game-dealer who pays a farmer for permission
to kill ground game and takes the game as his perqui-
site, is ' a person *bonâ fide* employed for reward,' asked
the magistrates to state a case for a superior court.
This they declined to do, their view being that no
question of law arose, but only an issue of fact, of
' written authority' or otherwise. Defendants then
moved for a rule for a *mandamus* requiring the magistrates to state a case, and the motion was argued before
the Divisional Court (Justices Hawkins and Wills) on
February 4, 1892. The Court held that the magistrates had decided the case upon an issue of *fact*, viz :
whether the ' occupier' had statutably employed the
defendants, and that they had evidence before them
upon which they could arrive at a conclusion in the
matter. They accordingly refused the application and
thereby supported the conviction.[2]

[1] Reported in *The Field*, November 4, 1891
[2] *The Field*, February 13, 1892.

As to what constitutes a 'resident on the land' (sect. 1 b.) the word 'reside' has been held to mean 'eat, drink, and sleep,'[1] and therefore, although a person merely spending the day would *not* be a resident, a guest for a few days presumably *might be*. In the case of Stuart *v.* Murray, the Court of Justiciary in Scotland decided that a person *bonâ fide* invited to stay for a week was a member of the household resident on the land.[2]

The question what constitutes a 'professional rabbit-killer' is also one that often arises. Subsection 1 b. states that he must be 'a person *bonâ fide* employed for reward,' and only one such person can be authorised at a time. This definition does not cover the case of a friend coming for a day's shooting, even if he receive a nominal sum for his services or a present of rabbits, although the fact of the shooter being a friend of the occupier would not necessarily invalidate the authority. Still, in the event of a shooting tenant feeling himself aggrieved and taking proceedings against such a person on the ground that he was not '*bonâ fide* employed for reward,' the fact of the latter being a friend of the occupier would not unnaturally give rise to suspicion.

[1] Regina *v.* North Curry, 4 B. & C. 959.
[2] *The Field*, November 22, 1894.

To take the case of a person who is not a friend of the occupier, and is not a rabbit-killer by profession, but (as if he were) enters into an agreement with the occupier to kill rabbits, ostensibly for reward but in reality for his own recreation :

In January 1893 one Gibbs, a wholesale confectioner at Oxford, was found by a keeper of the Earl of Abingdon shooting rabbits at Cumnor, on land in the occupation of one Townsend. He was summoned for trespass in pursuit of game, and pleaded that he had entered into an agreement with Townsend to kill rabbits for him, and to be paid for the work. Townsend confirmed this, and a written authority was produced showing that he was to be paid 4s. a dozen for all rabbits he killed up to September 29, and after that date 2s. a dozen, the rabbits being given to Townsend. The question arose whether Gibbs, who had a large business of his own in Oxford with several shops to look after, could be regarded as a 'professional rabbit-killer' within the meaning of the Act? The magistrates on the evidence dismissed the case, reluctantly finding him qualified! It is, of course, difficult to understand a man in defendant's position posing as a professional rabbit-killer ; but it is a free country, and if a man of means chooses to turn professional rabbit-killer there is no law to prevent him. At the same time, cases of this kind are open to grave suspicion, and slight evidence of an intention to evade the Act and obtain a few days' shooting on pretence of killing the rabbits for the benefit of the tenant, might warrant a conviction for trespass in pursuit of game. And this was the result in a similar case tried in another county.

In January 1883 the magistrates at Otley, Yorkshire, had a case before them, Taylor *v.* Bradley, in which this question was raised. The plaintiff, who was the shooting tenant over lands in the occupation of one Laycock, summoned the defendant (a nail manufacturer employing about twenty hands) for shooting rabbits on the said land. Defendant produced an authority in writing from the occupier Laycock, and the latter stated in evidence that he paid defendant five shillings for his services, and presented him with a rabbit. The question raised was whether Bradley was a person *bonâ fide* employed for reward for the purpose of killing ground game. The magistrates decided that he was not, and fined him 20*s.* and costs.

As to the formal appointment of a professional rabbit-killer, it may happen that a farmer is the 'occupier' of two or more farms belonging to one owner, and may be in doubt whether he can appoint one professional rabbit-killer for each farm, or whether his right is limited under the Act to the appointment of only one such person. We are not aware that this point has ever been decided in a court of law. It would probably depend whether all the farms were included in one lease and treated as one holding, or let under different leases. In the latter case it would probably be held that he may appoint as many persons as there are farms in his occupation.

The 'form' of authority to be given in writing is not provided by the Act. The following may be suggested as sufficient for the purpose:

'In pursuance of the provisions of the Ground Game Act 1880, I, A.B. of (give address), hereby authorise C. D. ('a member of my household, in my service,' or 'resident on the land in my occupation,' as the case may be) to kill or take ground game for me on any part of the land in my occupation in any lawful manner,[1] except by shooting.

'Dated this   day of   1898.

(Signed) A. B.'

If the occupier intends to authorise shooting, the form may be varied thus: 'to kill or take ground game by shooting, in the daytime only.'

[1] Poison is declared to be unlawful by Section 6.

This authority when given must be produced by the holder at any time when demanded by any person authorised to require its production.

A commoner is not an 'occupier' within the meaning of the Act; in other words, the right of common does not give or include any right to kill or take ground game.[1] Subsection 2 runs :

'A person shall not be deemed to be an occupier of land for the purposes of this Act by reason of his having a right of common over such lands ; or by reason of an occupation for the purpose of grazing or pasturage of sheep, cattle, or horses for not more than nine months.'

A commoner may maintain an action against the lord of a manor for surcharging it with coneys, but he has no right to kill them or to fill up the burrows.[2]

In view of the latter half of this subsection, owner in occupation who wishes to keep the shooting in his own hands, but is willing to let the grass lands for grazing purposes, should take care to stipulate in a written agreement that the letting is for a term not exceeding nine months. Otherwise the grazier might claim a concurrent right to the ground game as an 'occupier,' and would be justified in so doing,

[1] See Watkin *v.* Major, L.R. 10 C.P. 662
[2] Cooper *v.* Marshall, 1 Burr, 259.

under the Act. So if an owner in occupation lets his shooting to one person and the grazing to another, he should observe the same precautions.

Subsection 3 relates to moorlands :

' In the case of moorlands, and uninclosed lands (not being arable lands), the occupier and the persons authorised by him shall exercise the rights conferred by this section only from the eleventh day of December in one year until the thirty-first day of March in the next year, both inclusive ; but this provision shall not apply to detached portions of moorlands or uninclosed lands adjoining arable lands, where such detached portions of moorlands or uninclosed lands are less than twenty-five acres in extent.'

This clause applies more especially to grouse moors on which the occupier's right to kill hares and rabbits is limited to about four months in the year (unless the occupier happens to be the owner in possession), namely, from the last day of grouse shooting until the beginning of the nesting season. But on small outlying patches of moorland holding rabbits which might do damage on adjoining arable land, the ' occupier' is empowered to kill ground game all the year round.

Whether a farmer who has the grazing of moorland

for a period of *more* than nine months, but has a right to kill the ground game only from December 11 until March 31, can claim compensation for damage done by rabbits during the remainder of the year, is a question which, so far as we are aware, has not been decided in a court of law, but we are inclined to think that such a claim would be well founded.

A correspondent of *The Field* some time since put the following case under this section :

' How would large tracts of downland with much gorse, in some instances more than 100 acres in extent, be considered ?   Would they come under sect. 1, subsect. 3 of the Ground Game Act, and be considered for shooting purposes as "moorlands" ?

' They can scarcely be considered, "uninclosed" here, for they are generally surrounded by fences. They are essentially grazing lands, being fed by sheep, the fences being required to keep them in.   They are never ploughed, and, in some instances, are of very large extent.

' It would seem to the ordinary mind that the farmer, as " occupier," should not shoot such tracts of land, or snare, trap, or in any way kill or take ground game before December 11 on such downland.   Here, however, the farmer invariably shoots the downland as early as he pleases.   Is this within his right ? '

As this is a typical case we append the reply which was given to the question : [1]

'From the wording of the third subsection of Section 1 of the Act, which empowers an occupier, and those authorised by him, to exercise the rights conferred upon the moorlands and uninclosed lands (not being arable land) only from the end of grouse shooting (December 10) until the following March 31 —it seems clear that it is designed chiefly to prevent the disturbance of grouse during the nesting season ; and it is expressly stated that this provision is not to apply to detached portions of moorlands, or uninclosed lands adjoining arable lands, if they are less than 25 acres in extent. In the case stated by our correspondent, the land in question is not moorland within the meaning of the Act ; consequently, there can be no limitation of the time within which the ground game may be killed by those entitled to it, and if it were uninclosed, and less than 25 acres in extent, the occupier might kill or take the ground game there throughout the year. But it is said to be inclosed, and to be considerably more than 25 acres in extent, and consequently the case does not come within the third subsection at all. It is rather to be governed by the second subsection immediately preceding it, which

[1] *The Field*, November 3, 1894.

O

enacts that a person shall not be deemed an "occupier" by reason of his having a right of common over such lands; or by reason of an occupation for grazing purposes for not more than nine months. Now, if the land in question is downland, over which the farmer has a "right of common," and it is merely enclosed with a wire fence, as many such lands are, to prevent the sheep from straying, we should say that the farmer has no right whatever to the ground game. On the other hand, if he is an occupier for the purpose of grazing sheep, he can only kill or take ground game if his tenancy is for a longer period than nine months. In this case it would follow that, if our correspondent wishes to keep the rabbit shooting in his own hands, he must take care to let the grazing for short periods of not more than nine months.'

The *second* section of the Act provides that an occupier, who is entitled to kill ground game on land in his occupation, cannot divest himself wholly of such right. If he holds under a lease dated prior to September, 1880, and the game has not been reserved to the owner, he has an exclusive right to game both furred and feathered, and can let that exclusive right to anyone he pleases. But, if his tenancy has been created since that date without any reservation of the game, he cannot let such right in its entirety, but only a right to the feathered game with a partial right to the ground game, for as 'occupier' he is bound (under this section of the Act) not to divest himself wholly of his right to kill the hares and rabbits, however willing he may be to do so. All he can do is to refrain from exercising this inalienable right.

The *third* section of the Act accordingly provides that any agreement in contravention of the occupier's right to kill ground game would be void ; that is to say, that no such agreement could be enforced in a court of law if either of the parties happened to change his mind and refused to fulfil his contract. In the case of Hicks *v.* Smith, tried in the Cheltenham County Court in February, 1888, the defendant, an occupier of land in Gloucestershire, let to the plaintiff as shooting tenant an *exclusive* right to kill game and rabbits, and afterwards proceeded to snare rabbits himself. The plaintiff brought an action for breach of contract, and the defendant pleaded that the agreement was void under Section 3 of the Act. It was held that both parties were *in pari delicto*, the plaintiff knowing from the first that he was entering into an agreement that would be void under the Statute, and judgment accordingly was entered for the defendant.[1] A similar view was taken by the judge of the County Court at

---

[1] *The Field*, February 25, 1888.

Monmouth, in deciding the converse case of Morgan
v. Jackson, where an occupier brought an action to
recover rent from a shooting tenant to whom he had
let his right to the ground game, and who pleaded in
defence that the contract was void under Section 3 of
the Act. On appeal, however, to the Divisional Court
of Queen's Bench, it was held by Mr. Justice Day and
Mr. Justice Wright, that Section 3 was intended only
to prevent a tenant and landlord from combining together to defeat the Act. There was nothing in that
section (they said) to prevent the tenant (who was entitled otherwise than in pursuance of the Act to kill
and take ground game) being just as free as he would
have been before the Act, and, in their opinion, Section 3 did not apply, since it merely prevented a
tenant from surrendering his right to his landlord.[1]

It is curious that the limitation here given by the
judges—that Section 3 was only intended to prevent
collusion between landlord and tenant—was expressly
considered when the Bill was in Committee. Mr.
Chaplin moved to give the occupier of land of which
he was also the owner, power to sublet ; but Sir
William Harcourt said he could not consent to allow
the right to kill ground game to be separable from the
occupation of the land. Mr. Chaplin afterwards moved

[1] Reported in *The Field*, February 23, and May 4, 1895.

to give the tenant power to sublet the ground game ; but Sir William Harcourt maintained that this would defeat the object of the Bill, by enabling the tenant to let to the landlord. Another member then suggested that the tenant should have the power to let to *any other person than the landlord*, but Sir William Harcourt replied that he could not assent to so invidious a distinction. Now, however, it has been held by a Court of Appeal that there *is* such an invidious limitation (when the occupier is entitled to sporting rights otherwise than in pursuance of the Act), although it is not expressly mentioned in the Statute.

The position, therefore, seems to be that an occupier of lands owning the exclusive right to the ground game (as when a landlord in letting has not reserved the game and rabbits) may let the sporting rights and recover the rent, if his tenant is not his landlord. If his shooting tenant were also his landlord, the Court might possibly hold the contract void, and the rent irrecoverable—certainly a curious state of things. But in either case the occupier who is exclusive owner of sporting rights cannot divest himself of his concurrent right to kill the ground game, and while nominally letting the exclusive right, he, literally speaking, lets only the concurrent right, so far as the ground game is concerned.

An application for leave to appeal (which had been
refused by the Divisional Court) was made in the
Court of Appeal before the Master of the Rolls, and
Lord Justices Kay and A. L. Smith (July 22, 1895),
and was again refused. Accordingly, the position of
the occupier as above explained remains unaltered.
In other words, as settled by the Divisional Court,
an occupier under the Ground Game Act, although
unable to divest himself of his right to kill ground
game in favour of his landlord, may do so for money
value, or rent, in favour of *any other person*, and an
agreement in writing to that effect would *not* be void
under the third section of the Act.

The *fourth* section provides that a game licence is
not required for killing ground game under this Act,
but that, in pursuance of the Gun Licence Act, 1870,[1]
a ten-shilling 'gun licence' must be taken out by
every one who intends to kill ground game with firearms—unless, of course, he is already provided with a
game licence.

Under this section a variety of points arise.
Assuming that it applies only to 'owners' and
'occupiers'—as is clear from the words 'nothing in
this Act contained shall exempt *any person* from the
provisions of the Gun Licence Act, 1870'—what is

[1] 33 & 34 Vict. cap. 57.

the position (as regards a licence) of a person who is neither 'owner' nor 'occupier,' but who is, for example, an invited guest of the owner, or of the shooting tenant, or has permission to go over land by himself for the purpose of shooting rabbits only? Is he bound to take out a game licence (though not intending to shoot feathered game, or hares), or will a ten-shilling gun licence suffice? Before this point can be determined it is necessary to look at the provisions of no less than four statutes.[1]

The principal Game Act in defining 'game' does not include *rabbits*, woodcock, snipe, quail, or land rail. Consequently it is not an offence under that Act (Section 23) to kill rabbits without a licence. But Section 4 of the Game Licences Act, 1860 (23 & 24 Vict. cap. 90) runs thus:—

'Every person before he shall take, kill, or pursue . . . or use any dog, gun, net, or other engine for the purpose of taking, killing, or pursuing any *game*, or any woodcock, snipe, quail, landrail, *coney*, or deer, shall take out a proper licence to kill *game* under this Act . . . or forfeit 20*l*.'

In other words, under the Game Licences Act,

---

[1] The principal Game Act, 1 & 2 Will. IV. cap. 32; the Game Licences Act, 1860; the Gun Licence Act, 1870; and the Ground Game Act, 1880.

1860, a game licence is required to kill rabbits, although they are not 'game.' But certain persons are named to whom this does not apply, and rabbits may be killed without a game licence 'by the proprietor of any warren, or enclosed ground, or by the tenant of lands either by himself, or by his direction, or permission.'

The Gun Licence Act, 1870, provides that everyone 'who shall use or carry a gun,' no matter for what purpose, shall take out a ten-shilling licence under a penalty of ten pounds; while the Ground Game Act, 1880, as we have seen, declares that a ten-shilling licence is required for killing ground game.

The net result of these various enactments appears to be that, while the holder of a game licence may kill any kind of game, as well as rabbits, woodcock, snipe, &c., a person who intends to confine his attention to rabbits may shoot them if holding a ten-shilling licence only.[1] In connection with this subject a curious point was recently raised, and only decided after two appeals, *à propos* of rabbits and the Gun Licence Act, the principal provision of which has been already stated. By the terms of this Act certain persons are exempted from taking out a gun licence,

---

[1] Both owners and occupiers may kill hares without a licence under the provisions of the Hares Act, 1848, and may authorise others to do so for them.

JUST MISSED HIM

and amongst others ' the occupier (or his nominee) of any lands using or carrying a gun for the purpose of scaring birds, or *killing vermin.*' A Scottish farmer who, from an agriculturist's point of view, regarded rabbits as vermin, resisted payment of the gun licence on the ground that he came within this exemption. He was summoned before the Sheriff at Cupar, who, after hearing the case argued, decided that rabbits were *not* ' vermin.' From this decision the farmer appealed, and in February, 1898, Lord Stormonth-Darling, considering himself bound by precedent (Gosling *v.* Brown, 1878, 5 R. 755), though against his better judgment, reversed the Sheriff's finding, and decided that rabbits *were* vermin, and that the farmer was accordingly exempt from taxation. This verdict was once more challenged, and the full Court of Appeal in Edinburgh, a month later, reversed Lord Stormonth-Darling's decision, and, supporting the Sheriff's opinion, held that rabbits were *not* vermin.[1] It is now therefore conclusively settled that rabbits are not ' vermin' within the meaning of the Gun Licence Act, 1870, and that a ten-shilling licence is required for shooting them.

It may be here observed that the term ' gun' includes a firearm of any description, and an air-gun,

[1] See *The Field* of March 5 and April 2, 1898.

or any other kind of gun from which any shot, bullet, or other missile can be discharged. Even a toy pistol has been held to be a gun.[1] A catapult, of course, is not 'a firearm,' and although it may 'discharge a shot, bullet, or other missile,' it can hardly be called a 'gun.' If, instead of the words 'or any other kind of gun,' the statute were to read 'or any other engine,' a catapult would come within the definition.

To return to the Ground Game Act :

The *fifth* section provides that an 'occupier' cannot exercise his concurrent right to the ground game if the right to kill or take it has been already vested in some one else by lease dated prior to the passing of this Act. An important decision upon this section was given in the case of Allhusen *v.* Brooking by Mr. Justice Chitty,[2] who held that it extended to an agreement dated prior to the Act, whereby a lessor agreed to grant a lease for a term to commence after the passing of the Act, and the tenant was restrained from killing ground game otherwise than as provided by the terms of his agreement.

[1] See Campbell *v.* Hadley, 40 J.P. 756 ; and for further convictions for using a pistol without a licence, see *The Field*, April 10 and 17, 1897, and June 18, 1898.

[2] 51 Law Times Reports, N.S. 57. See also Hassard *v* Clark, 13 L. Rep. Irish Ch. Div., 391

It is further enacted by this section that :

'Nothing in this Act shall affect any special right of killing or taking ground game to which any person other than the landlord, lessor, or occupier may have become entitled before the passing of this Act by virtue of any franchise, charter, or Act of Parliament.'

This is a very important provision, since it defeats the right of an 'occupier' to kill ground game if the land in his occupation happens to be land over which a right of free warren is claimed. We have already alluded to this contingency in the chapter on warrens, where we have cited, by way of illustration (pp. 55, 56), the typical case of Lord Carnarvon *v.* Clarkson, which see.

The *sixth* section of the Act prohibits the shooting of ground game *by night*, setting spring traps anywhere except in rabbit holes, and employing poison.

The question has arisen whether this section—particularly the prohibition as to spring traps—applies to owners who are in occupation of their own land. The point was raised and decided in the case of Smith *v.* Hunt,[1] which came before the magistrates at Worcester in 1885. It was contended on the part of the prosecution that the Act applied to *all* persons having the right of killing ground game, including

[1] 54 Law Times Reports, p. 422.

owners occupying their own land, and on the part of the defendant (an owner) it was urged that the Act applied to occupiers only. The magistrates were unable to agree as to the true construction of the section, and decided to dismiss the summons, and state a case for the opinion of a superior court. Accordingly in the Queen's Bench Division on November 26, 1885, before Justices Mathew and Smith, the case came on for argument, when the appeal was dismissed with costs, the judges being of opinion that Section 6 of the Act does *not* apply to owners who occupy their own land.

It is a well-known principle in courts of justice that the meaning of an Act of Parliament must be based upon the *wording* of the Act, and not upon the supposed *intention* of those who framed it. Nevertheless, it is curious that judges so frequently refer to what they consider the manifest intention of the Legislature, and yet give a construction that is very different from what was explained in Parliament.

So in the present case, Mr. Justice Mathew observed : 'I think it is clear from the wording of the Act alone, that the Legislature had no intention of restricting the undoubted rights which landlords possessed before the Act was passed to deal with their land and kill the game thereon in any way they liked.'

That this was not the intention of the Legislature may be seen from the report of the debates during the progress of the Bill through Committee. The clause relating to spring traps originally stood thus : ' Neither such occupier nor any person authorised by him shall employ spring traps above ground for the purpose of killing ground game.' Had the Bill been passed in that form the limitation in the use of spring traps would, of course, not have applied to landlords; but Mr. Gregory moved an amendment altering the clause to ' no person having a right of killing ground game *under this Act or otherwise* ; ' on which the Home Secretary, Sir William Harcourt, observed that, ' Seeing that the amendment *placed the landlord and tenant on the same footing,* he was willing to accept it.' It passed accordingly ; and what was afterwards Sir William Harcourt's view as to the meaning of the law which he was so instrumental in getting passed, is shown by what he stated in the House of Commons in May, 1883, in reply to Sir A. Gordon, who inquired whether Her Majesty's Government would move Parliament to restore in Scotland the liberty to use spring traps in rabbit runs, of which they have been deprived by the Ground Game Act. Sir William Harcourt said, ' It did not really take away from the tenant farmers anything which as a right they enjoyed (i.e. before the passing of the Act), because under the terms of their leases they were prohibited from killing game in any way whatever. But during the progress of the Bill it was represented to him that other persons were allowed to set spring traps, and in this way they could kill a great many things besides rabbits. It seemed to him that spring traps were cruel things, and he intended to limit the use of spring traps not against tenants only, but against *everybody*. Nobody was allowed, *whether proprietor or tenant*, to set a spring trap in the open, and for this reason, that it killed a great many animals that it was not desired to kill.'

Thus it is clear that the construction placed upon the sixth section of the Act by the Justices of Appeal in Smith *v.* Hunt is not in accordance with the expressed intention of the Government as stated by Sir William Harcourt.

Nevertheless their decision has been followed in the case of McMahon *v.* Hannon, which came before the Exchequer Division, Dublin, on May 15, 1888, by way of appeal on a case stated by the Justices of the Co. Clare, sitting at Dunass. The Lord Chief Baron and Mr. Justice Andrews were of opinion that the sixth section of the Act did not apply to owners of land in fee simple in possession, but only to occupiers not in fee simple. From this view Baron Dowse dissented.[1]

The decision in these two cases, which had reference to spring traps only, will of course apply equally to the use of poison, and to shooting at night, as all are included in the same section. It would follow, also, that a sporting tenant who rents the shooting from an owner in occupation, will, in regard to Section 6 of the Act, be in the position of the owner.

Under Section 7, a person (e.g. an ordinary shooting tenant) who is not in occupation of the land, but has the sole right of killing the game thereon—subject to the concurrent right of the 'occupier' to the ground game—has as much authority to institute legal proceedings as if he were exclusive owner, without prejudice of course to the right of the occupier.

The *eighth* section of the Act defines the words 'ground game' to mean 'Hares and Rabbits.'

The *ninth* section provides that a person acting in conformity with this statute shall not thereby be

[1] Reported in *The Field* of May 26, 1888. See also the case of Saunders *v.* Pitfield, which came before the Divisional Court by way of appeal from the magistrates at Bishop's Lydeard, Somerset. In this case the defendant claimed, as tenant from year to year under an agreement, made prior to the Act, in which there was no reservation of shooting rights to the lessor, and the magistrates decided that the Act did not apply. The Court of Appeal decided otherwise. See *The Field*, January 28, 1888.

subject to any proceedings or penalties in pursuance of any other statute. For example, if under this Act he were to take out a ten-shilling gun licence and proceed to shoot rabbits, he could not be prosecuted under the Game Licences Act 1860, for shooting rabbits without a game licence.

The *tenth* section has reference to the killing of ground game on days on which under other statutes the killing of game is prohibited (as for example on a Sunday or on Christmas Day, or at night), and is to be read in harmony with such statutes.

Although rabbits may be killed all the year round, there is no close time for hares except Sundays and Christmas Day, when no dog, gun, net or other engine may be used to take them (1 & 2 Will. IV. cap. 32).

The Hares Preservation Act of 1892, however, makes it illegal to *sell* or *expose for sale* any hare or leveret during the months of March, April, May, June or July, although this does not apply to foreign hares which may have been imported. The marked omission of the word 'kill' in a statute framed ostensibly for the purpose of *preserving* hares, will probably strike most people as a *reductio ad absurdum*. In Ireland, however, by 42 & 43 Vict., c. 23, no one may kill or take a hare between April 20 and

August 12, under a penalty of 20*s.* ; and in many counties this close time has since been varied by the Lord Lieutenant on application of the Grand Juries, so as to extend from April 1 to August 12.

If a snare be set on a Saturday and game be caught on Sunday, it is deemed to be used on Sunday within the meaning of the Act, and the person setting it is liable to a penalty, though he may not have been on the land on Sunday.[1]

The *eleventh* and last section gives the short title of the Act and is as follows :—' This Act may be cited for all purposes as the Ground Game Act 1880.'

Various points from time to time arise which, although outside the direct wording of the Act, are nevertheless more or less connected with points expressly governed by it. For example, the question sometimes arises whether an ' owner ' has the right to ferret rabbits on the land which he has let to the ' occupier.' The farmer will maintain that he has not, and that he can only kill the ground game when out shooting. But the farmer is wrong. An ' occupier ' has no monopoly of any particular method of capture conferred on him by the Ground Game Act. He has merely a concurrent right to kill the hares and rabbits on the land in his occupation, and the landlord

[1] Allen *v.* Thompson, L.R. 5 Q.B. 336 ; 22 L.T. 472.

P

retains a similar right. Both may employ dogs, ferrets, traps, nets, and snares; in fact, whatever method is legal to the one is legal to the other, unless the Act states otherwise. The fact that no mention of 'ferreting' is made in the Act shows that the right remains unaltered; for if the landlord had been deprived of such right, the Act would have stated it in express terms.

When an 'owner' has let his shooting for a term, he must be careful not to let before the expiration of that term any portion of the same land to an agricultural tenant who might claim as 'occupier' a right to kill the ground game. This happened in the case of Reade *v.* Whitmore where a shooting tenant under these circumstances brought an action against the owner for breach of implied covenant for quiet enjoyment, and the Court decided in his favour.[1]

This shows the necessity, when letting shooting rights, of having a clear understanding as to the ground game; and an owner who may contemplate a subsequent letting of some or all of the land for agricultural purposes should expressly stipulate with the shooting tenant that such letting shall not be deemed a breach of contract. The shooting tenant, on the other hand, should ascertain whether the land

[1] *The Field*, April 25, 1891.

is, or is not, in the owner's occupation, and if it is, should see that his agreement specifies the sum which is to be allowed off the rent in the event of any portion being subsequently let. Of course if the tenant agrees to the landlord's proviso, that any such letting for agricultural purposes is not to be deemed a breach of contract, no claim for reduction of rent can arise.

When commenting on Section 7 of the Act (p. 207) we referred to the power of a shooting tenant to institute legal proceedings as if he were owner. It is important to note that when a right of shooting is let, the agreement between the parties should be *in writing under hand and seal.* A mere letter, such as would suffice in an ordinary case of bargain or sale, will not answer the purpose; for the right of sporting is 'an incorporeal hereditament,' for the legal transfer of which a formal deed is necessary, and without this neither the lessor nor the lessee, in case of dispute, would be able to enforce his right. It is true that a simple permission in writing (for example by letter) would be sufficient authority to the holder for merely shooting over the ground; but it would not enable him to prosecute trespassers in pursuit of game, nor to do any other act which is exercisable only by an owner. Half the disputes which arise over shooting agreements are generally due to a disregard of this precaution.

The patient reader who has followed us thus far will probably be of opinion that, although this lengthy chapter may even now be not quite exhaustive of the subject, for most practical purposes, perhaps, enough has been written. We need only add that a copy of 'The Ground Game Act' costs but three-halfpence, and may be obtained from the Queen's Printers, Messrs. Eyre & Spottiswoode, East Harding Street, Fetter Lane, E.C.

CHAPTER VIII

RABBIT-HAWKING WITH THE GOSHAWK

IN foregoing chapters some account has been given
of the various ways of taking rabbits by netting,
snaring, ferreting, and shooting, each of which will
commend itself differently to different readers according to their respective tastes. There remains yet
another phase of sport to be described ; and although
in reality a very ancient one, it will probably appear
to most people both novel and attractive. We refer
to the art of taking rabbits with a trained goshawk.
We find both rabbit and goshawk (as well as ferret)
mentioned in the Book of St. Albans, 1486, and
learn from that very curious compilation the technical
terms which were expected to be known by 'gentyl-
men and honeste persones in comunynge of theyr
hawkes,' and other animals. For instance, when
referring to *old* rabbits it was customary to speak of a

'bury of coneys,' or if *young*, 'a nest of rabbettes.' [1]
The sportsman found a coney 'syttynge,' and when
killed, it was not skinned but 'unlacyd,' while the
warrener's useful four-footed allies were referred to as
a 'besynesse of ferettes'—all very quaint, though the
sport itself was pretty much the same then as now.

Rabbit-hawking has much to recommend it. It
is not difficult to carry out in an enclosed country
where long-winged hawks cannot be flown; it is an
effective mode of keeping down the stock of rabbits
in places where they are apt to become too numerous;
it may be practised at any season of the year, and, as
it may be pursued without any noise, it does not, like
shooting, disturb the winged game. As to the sport
which it affords to those who participate in it, *experto
crede.*

The first thing to be done, of course, is to procure
a goshawk, and for this one must send to France or
Germany. It is very many years since a goshawk's
nest was found in Great Britain; not since Colonel
Thornton, of Thornville Royal, Yorkshire, a keen
falconer and good all-round sportsman, discovered
one in the forest of Rothiemurcus and trained one of
the young birds. This was at the end of the last, or

[1] See our remarks on the original application of the word
rabbit, p. 4.

beginning of the present century, since which time no similar discovery has been recorded. The goshawks trained and flown in England at the present day (and we know of many) are procured from France or Germany; chiefly from France, where, thanks to the good offices of some of the French falconers, they are annually looked after, the nests protected, and the young birds secured at the proper season. The price varies with the age and condition of the bird. You may get one through a German dealer for a couple of pounds, but it will be a chance whether the flight feathers will be unbroken, and perfect wings are a *sine quâ non* in the case of a hawk that is to be trained and flown. It is better to pay a little more, as at the Jardin d'Acclimatation in Paris, and secure a good one. Occasionally a goshawk is taken in a bow-net by one of the Dutch hawk-catchers at Valkenswaard in North Brabant, and is sent to England with the falcons which are annually forwarded in autumn to the members of the Old Hawking Club and others; but as a rule the birds captured there are peregrines, for which at the present day there is greater demand.

As to the mode of training, if the purchaser of a goshawk has never handled a hawk before, and knows nothing of the matter, he will do well to provide himself with some modern treatise on the subject (such as 'Hints on the Management of Hawks,' published at *The Field* office), wherein he will learn the rudiments of falconry, and find a special chapter on the goshawk. If he wishes to find real enjoyment in the sport, he must train the bird himself, and not depute it to another. A hawk must learn to know her owner, or she will not allow him to take her up when she has killed her quarry. She must be fed by him; carried by him on the glove as much as possible, bare-headed, that is unhooded, to accustom her to the sight of men and dogs, that she may put off all fear and become as fond of him as a dog would be, knowing his voice and obeying his call, or 'lure.'

Supposing that the hawk has had put on the legs, just above the feet, 'jesses' (or little leather straps) by which she is held, to the ends of which are attached the 'swivel' and 'leash' by means of which she is tethered to the 'perch' or 'block,' the first step is to get her to come off the perch on to the glove to be fed; and this is accomplished by offering a little bit of meat, or the leg of a fowl, or rabbit. When she will step readily on to the fist, the leash being untied, the distance should be increased from a foot to a yard, and at length to several yards, until eventually she will fly willingly across the room to her master.

This lesson being repeated out of doors from a field-gate, or the top of a stone wall, while for safety a long line is attached to the swivel, she will in a few days come readily when 'called off,' and the line may then be discarded.

She may then be lured with a dead rabbit, or a part of one, thrown down and drawn with a string along the grass. After coming readily to this several times, she is next to be 'entered' to the live quarry. For this purpose a young rabbit or two may be easily procured by ferreting, and being placed under an inverted flower-pot which can be pulled over from a distance with a piece of string and a cross-stick through the hole in the bottom, the hawk is slipped at the right moment, and rarely fails to take the rabbit at the first attempt. Another trial or two of this kind, and she is ready to fly at a wild one. The critical part of the training is now at hand, and great care must be taken to avoid disappointing the hawk; that is to say, the rabbit should be well in the open, and not within reach of a hedgerow or burrow into which it may pop just as the hawk is about to seize it. It must be remembered, says Capt. F. H. Salvin, who has paid much attention to the goshawk, that one great point in the successful training of all young hawks is to avoid, as far as possible, disappointment in their early attempts. This necessitates the sacrifice of some few unfortunate birds or beasts, which have no chance of escape given to them, but is in reality little more than what other sports demand, such as cub-hunting, and the numbers of young grouse or other game annually sacrificed in the process of dog-breaking before the commencement of the shooting season. A small stock of rabbits, say four or five, had better be caught for the purpose of 'entering.' As soon as a goshawk will take these rabbits in a 'creance' (or long line) she may be considered ready for the field. Encouraged by the success of these first attempts, she will go on improving every day, and the more she is carried and flown the better she will become.

The worst fault which a goshawk possesses is that of 'taking stand,' that is, perching on a tree in order to command a good position when the game is put up. Unless very keen, a hawk in this position will refuse to come down to the 'lure,' and will obstinately sit still, looking in all directions for the quarry. For this reason it is a good plan to begin the training on open ground destitute of trees.

Some persons are under the impression that flying a trained hawk on a manor must tend to drive the game away; but this is not the case. It has been conclusively shown elsewhere [1] that flying falcons at grouse does not spoil the moor for shooting, and it is the same with the goshawk when flown at rabbits. All is done so quietly, that one may capture a dozen rabbits in an afternoon without disturbing the game half so much as if a dozen shots were fired. On this question the following letter, received from one who has tried it, is to the point: ' Having enjoyed four seasons' hawking with a well-known sportsman, who has about 5,000 acres of shooting, I have heard it said by many, and have noticed it myself, that we found more game on ground where we had had three seasons' hawking, than on those portions of the farm where we could not hawk. I hope the good old sport will increase.'

To show what success may be attained even in the first season with a young goshawk, we may refer to the bag made by a falconer still living. In his first season with a young female goshawk (better than a male because larger and stronger) he took 322 rabbits, 3 hares, and 2 magpies, and the following season 280 rabbits, 2 leverets, 11 partridges, 4 magpies, and 2 squirrels.

A well-trained goshawk, belonging to Mr. John

[1] *Hints on the Management of Hawks*, second edition, 1898, pp. 89–92.

Riley, of Putley Court, Herefordshire, took 70 rabbits
in fifteen days, killing 10 on her best day. This was
in her third season. In her first year she took 110
rabbits, 2 pheasants, 13 water-hens, and 1 rat; in her
second season 130 rabbits, 1 pheasant, 3 water-hens,
and 1 stoat. The same falconer trained a male goshawk, which in his first season took 26 partridges,
10 pheasants, 16 rabbits, 5 landrails, 12 water-hens,
and 1 stoat.

In *The Field* of May 2, 1896, Sir Henry Boynton,
of Burton Agnes, Hull, wrote as follows :

'It may interest some of your readers, who are
lovers of falconry, to learn what I have done with a
nestling goshawk which I brought from Nordland,
Norway, in June, 1895. She killed her first wild rabbit
on September 17. Her two best days were as follows :
the best 24 rabbits out of 24 flights ; the next best day
20 rabbits out of 24 flights. The hawk had throughout the season, on an average, a three-quarter crop a
day, and was consequently in the very highest condition, which rendered her able to undergo the hardest
work that a hawk is capable of enduring. She was
flown on seventy days, and the total bag for the season
was : rabbits 407, hare 1, rats 5, stoat 1, weasel 1, total
415 head ; and every one of the quarry mentioned was
killed in fair flight, without being handled in any way.'

It is, of course, not to be supposed that the hawk will kill every time she is flown. The rabbit may get to ground, or into a hedgerow, before he is overtaken; and the owner, if he be wise, will not slip his hawk at a rabbit which is too near one or the other of such retreats. There should be plenty of room, and the longer the course the better for all concerned.

In the accompanying illustration it will be seen that a rabbit on being put up has made straight for a sandpit; the hawk might have seized him on the very edge of it, but just as she has clutched at him, he has leapt boldly down the steep bank, and in another second will be gone to ground'—

'Whoo-oop!'

CHAPTER IX

THE COOKERY OF THE RABBIT

By Alexander Innes Shand

THE rabbit is a most useful and respectable animal, yet his merits have been unfairly ignored, simply because he is cheap and common. Almost unknown to the *menus* of the modern *haute cuisine*, we suspect that, as the conger eel often does duty for turtle, he has figured anonymously in dishes of world-wide reputation. To take a single example : we have good reason to surmise that he often served for the foundation of the famous *potage à la Bagration*, the secret of which was religiously kept by the defunct Frères Provençaux of the Palais Royal. That most seductive of soups was supposed to be based upon sweetbreads or chicken. A casual indiscretion leads us to believe that the rabbit entered largely into its composition, but the invaluable recipe is probably irrecoverable. While the Provençal brothers flourished, and since their demise, ' Bagration ' has been paraded in many a bill of fare, but neither at the Old Philippe's, nor at the Café Anglais, nor at Bignon's have we ever recognised the genuine masterpiece.

The rabbit is cheap and common ; but he is growing in popularity, and is destined to cut a more conspicuous figure in the future than in the past. The old order is changing, and the subversive spirit of democracy is invading the game market. Prices are being levelled downwards ; the luxuries of the last generation are losing in consideration, and what used to be rarities have ceased to be rare. The finest park-fed venison seldom appears now at private tables, and such a thing as the exquisite saddle of roedeer, the favourite *Rehrücke* of the Germans, is never to be seen. As for the fore-quarters of the deer, they are become a mere drug in the market. The frugal housekeeper finds pheasants more economical than fowls, when the big shoots of the autumn are on ; and with the craze for deadly days, and the rivalry in record bags, they are likely in the future to sell as freely in the New Cut as in Bond Street. Moreover, British prejudices are breaking down, and year by by year the trade is growing in game from America and the Continent. It has been discovered that prairie-hens, hazel-hens, and the Russian and Scandinavian ptarmigan are very often excellent eating, though speculating in them is always something of a lottery. Every intelligent man knows that when he buys a 'Norfolk hare,' it has more probably been imported from Central Germany, nor is it any the worse for that. In short, each 'piece' of game begins to be taken on its merits, and when the rabbit has fair play with furred and feathered competitors, we are assured he must come to the front with the leaps and bounds which carry him out of the coverts into the sprouting wheat.

What is certain is that we shall always have him, not only in a sufficiency but in superabundance, and out of sheer charity to the farmers we are bound to consume him. Fortunately it is a case where philanthropy should coincide with inclination. The coop-bred pheasant is an artificial product, and might disappear with a change in sporting fashions. Sir William Harcourt has shown us that a caprice of the Legislature may well nigh exterminate the aboriginal hare. But we defy the most drastic Act of Parliament to set limits to the amazing fertility of the rabbit. He is as industrious in multiplying himself as the rat or the guinea-pig, and has resources in rendering himself a nuisance which challenge competition. He swarms everywhere in sandy or light soil, and even when he seeks his settlements in the stiffest clay, he scoops out sanctuaries in labyrinths of burrows. They tell us that he originally passed into tawny Spain from more torrid Africa, though as to whether he was introduced by the invading Arabs, swam the Straits, or passed through the submarine tunnel by which the monkeys came from Apes Hill to the Rock of Gibraltar, the soundest historians are not agreed. Be that as it may, it seems certain that Spain is his European *Stammland*, whence he has spread over all southern countries to the shores of the Ægean.

The Spaniards have always had him in high consideration. He is engraved on their ancient coins and medals, and we are told by Strabo that they used to consign him by shiploads to the Roman markets. 'Lord, what a draught London has!' exclaimed Scott in his diary, when he saw a fleet of Thames smacks fishing off Cape Wrath. But that was nothing to the draught of Republican or Imperial Rome, when a Lucullus or a Vitellius was ransacking the Roman world for luxuries. As there were no refrigerating chambers in those days, we can only suppose that live rabbits were stowed away in hutches. Considering the length and chances of the voyage, the freights could not have been low, and the rabbits must have been intended for the tables of the wealthy. And they must have been consigned very much out of condition, as the

natives dredged in the Colchester beds or the shell-fish
trapped off the Cornish tinneries. But in his native
Spain the rabbit is indeed a delicacy. Perhaps he
shows to the greater advantage by contrast; for the
beef is leather, and the mutton india-rubber. But the
rabbit fattens on the best grazing going, and the very
air he inhales is balm, among the wild thyme and
aromatic shrubs of the *dehesas* and *depoblados*. So
in a country where the game laws are laughed to
scorn, the muleteer or mounted wayfarer has always
the gun lying across the saddle bow, in readiness
for the snapshot. Then the rabbit is stuffed into the
mouth of the saddle bag, to be brought forth and
stewed down for the evening's *puchero*. But though it
is an agreeable variety on the rare scraps of rusty bacon
or the garlic-scented sausages, the frugal Spaniard
never hesitates to make merchandise of his prize.
Many a time has the forlorn Englishman, riding far
away from the lean larders of the *fondas*, and meditat-
ing ruefully on the doubtful chances of supper in
posada or *venta*, which only supplies shelter and fires,
had a pleasant awakening when he met some poaching
rascal with a rabbit or a brace of red-legged partridges
to sell. There was slight haggling over the blissful
bargain. And at nightfall, sitting over the smoulder-
ing charcoal fire, in the mixed group of muleteers

goatherds and mendicants, he could possess his soul
in patience and the savoury steam of the stew where
his rabbit was slowly simmering in the pipkin. The
pleasures of hope were tryingly prolonged, but there
was ample reward in the rich fruition. As we shall
remark, the rabbit is conspicuous in our literature by
its absence, but we have always marvelled that we
hear little or nothing of it either in ' Don Quixote ' or
' Gil Blas.' We know that the Governor of Barataria
was a gourmand, and the worthy Squire of the Knight-
errant, with the scent of an old dog fox, was the very
prince of foragers. What gastronomist can fail to
sympathise with his raptures when he exultingly
marked the cowheels for his own ? It was like coming
on a water spring in the wastes of the Sahara. And
as it is inconceivable that he never picked up rabbits
en route, we can only suppose that Cervantes had a
prejudice on the subject. Possibly he was surfeited
with rabbits when chained to the galley oars in Bar-
bary ; but we confess that that theory is on the face
of it improbable.

Borrow, although a militant envoy of the Bible
Society, inured to hard fare and rough quarters, had
a strong dash of the gourmet in the natural man.
We always remember with pleasure the unfeigned
enjoyment of Lavengro over the round of beef at the

coaching house on the western road, when he rose like
a giant refreshed at the invitation of the superstitious
squire to walk away to a second dinner. Riding
through the robber-haunted country from Lisbon
to Madrid, he arrived at the heaven-forsaken hamlet
of Pegoens. Expecting little, he was agreeably surprised in the miserable inn, which bore the ominous
sobriquet of 'The Hostelry of Thieves.' 'We had a
rabbit fried, the gravy of which was delicious, and
afterwards a roasted one, which was brought up on
a dish entire: the hostess having first washed her
hands, proceeded to tear the animal to pieces, which
having accomplished, she poured over the fragments
a sweet sauce. I ate heartily of both dishes, particularly of the last, owing perhaps to the novel and
curious manner in which it was served up.' That
semi-barbarous landlady knew what she was about,
for the fault of roasted rabbit is the dryness. The
fatless flesh parches in the cooking like the plains of
La Mancha in the summer droughts. But Pegoens
is in the very heart of a desolate country, where the
rabbits, sheltering from the circling birds of prey,
revel near the mouths of their burrows in the fragrant
undergrowth which supplies them at once with food
and protection. Borrow in his character of the
Romany Rye must have been skilled in the dressing

of the rabbit. For Mr. Petulengro and his other gypsy pals seldom take their strolls abroad without snares in their pockets : and where they bivouac the buries are laid under contribution. They have no objection to the pheasant or the fowl, but the rabbit in their *menus* ranks rather above the hare, and, in fact, comes only second to the hedgehog.

The rabbit followed the Saracen—or preceded him—into Sicily and Southern Italy ; for we have seen that he was imported as a foreign delicacy in the time of the old Romans. We can sympathise the more cordially with Borrow at Pegoens, that we remember a famous stew unexpectedly served to us at Calatafimi, when the Sicilian muleteer had gone on an unsuccessful foray, and came back with nothing but sausages and black bread. Fleas and mosquitos were busy that night, but, thanks to that supper, after the weary ride, sleep set them at defiance. We have seldom seen the rabbit in Naples. He was a luxury beyond the reach of the Lazzaroni, who live through the summer chiefly on water-melons, and in winter on the untempting circular *pizze*, apparently less nutritious than stale ship-biscuit. But he figures ostentatiously in the Roman markets, which are even more interesting to the naturalist and the student of national tastes than to the gourmet. The descendants of a noble race may have degenerated, but at least they are superior to vulgar prejudices. They have laid to heart one precept of their saintly patron, for they call nothing that is edible common or unclean. Go into the Piazza Navona, or any of the other markets, of a morning, before the cooks have done bargaining for the provision of the day, and you will see as miscellaneous an assortment of viands as may be met with anywhere. Rabbits and frogs, and not unfrequently cats, rub shoulders with quails, beccaficos, and ortolans. The famous Roman dinner at the Minerva, and, still more, an improvised luncheon at some *osteria* in the Campagna, used to be a triumph of gastronomic license. The comparatively rare porcupine took the *pas*; for the Romans are as devoted to that highly flavoured dainty as the Algerians and Kabyles; but the rabbits, spitted or stewed, were always among the *pièces de résistance.*

The motley morning spectacle in a Roman market[1] reminds us of a more æsthetic group, elaborated by Eugène Sue in the ‘ Gourmandise ’ of his ‘ Sept Péchés Capitaux.’ The Doctor Gasterini, in advocating the vice he maintains to be a virtue, leads his guest to the stall of his nephew, Léonard, the poacher. Léonard, with the inspiration of the sylvan artist, has arranged a game trophy; the wild boar and the deer are swinging from a tree trunk, and rabbits are festooned around, with wild geese, pheasants and red partridges. But the French, being a nation of cooks, have set a due value on their rabbits, and not a few of their novelists have delighted to do them honour. A *solide lapin* is a title of respect, bestowed by the reckless criminal class on some truculent athlete. Sue, in the 'Mystères de Paris,' makes the 'Lapin Blanc' the resort of his outcasts and ruffians. The outlawed poacher Bête-puante, in his 'Enfant Trouvé,' snares rabbits and tenches in the swamps where he goes to earth with the foxes and badgers. George Sand refers to the rabbit frequently in her romances of the desolate Sologne. We are somewhat surprised that Dumas makes no reference to him in 'Le Meneur de Loups,' where he passes most sorts of game under review. That explains itself, however ; for, as Thiébault hunted with a cortège of wolves, the rabbits scuttled to their burrows when they heard the pack giving tongue. Then there are the cockney or realistic novelists of France who leave the field and the forest for the city and the cooking range. The *gibelotte de lapin* is a standard *plat* at all the *bourgeois restaurants* of the banlieue and environs, from Boulogne to Vincennes and Enghien to Fontainebleau. Seldom is there a merry-making in Paul de Kock, Gaboriau, or Zola, but the hungry holiday-makers are looking out for the *gibelotte*. And there is the standard joke that the cat often does duty for his *confrère*, when the absence of the head excites suspicion. Though that is, of course, a calumny in most cases ; for cats are less easily come by than coneys.

In Belgium a profitable business is done in rabbit-breeding. Nothing except the rabbit of Spain can be superior to the wild rabbit of the Ardennes ; but the so-called Belgian hares which are reared in hutches have lost much of the savage flavour. Great pains is taken in rearing them ; they are a large and very prolific variety of what is virtually a rabbit. The hutches have projecting roofs to throw off the rain and are floored with wire gratings ; the rabbits are shifted twice or thrice a day; the young are soon separated from the mother, and killed under three months. Often as many as two hundred tons have been imported from Ostend in the cold season. Nevertheless the meat is insipid and does not commend itself to the connoisseur. With the perfection of refrigerating chambers, the importation from Australia and New Zealand has been increasing fast. That is so far satisfactory; but the rabbit threatens to be a curse to the distressed colonists. The enterprising gentlemen who sent over here for a few couples have pulled the string of an irrepressible douche bath. In the bracing climate and sandy soil, the new arrivals multiplied like fleas, and now they tell us that the supperless tramp has only to sit down quietly by the track-side for his supper to jump into his arms. And as mutton in Australasia is still almost a drug, the destructive rabbit is superfluous for home consumption. In England he will always find a ready market, though prices may fall with an excessive supply. There was a time, in the period of the carrier's cart and the sailing smack, when Scotch servants and retainers struck against the rabbits, as they did against the monotony of salmon and sea-trout. Nowadays, from the most northerly shootings, regular consignments are despatched to Liverpool or Hull, to be circulated through the mining districts and the Midlands. The rabbit has become a favourite food of the poorer classes, and all they have to learn is more appetising variety in cookery.

It is suggestive that the rabbit is scarcely mentioned in the English novel ; except, indeed, in those moral little tales where the virtuous peasant is first seduced into evil courses by snaring a hare or netting a rabbit for a sick wife, whence he passes on to the pot-house and the prison, and possibly to the gallows, after shooting a keeper. Scott, with his broad range

of the Buccleuch domains, made no account of such
small deer, and in the caldron which Meg Merrilies
cooked in the haunted Kaim of Derncleugh, there
were hares and moor game, and partridges, and everything else but rabbits. Even Richard Jefferies, who
can wax eloquent over a leg of mutton and mealy
potatoes, and who must many a day have dined off
rabbit on the Wiltshire Downs, ungratefully says not
a word of it in its gastronomical aspects. In fact,
the only allusion we can call to mind in the whole
range of English domestic fiction is when the osten-
tatious and parsimonious Jawleyford tells Mr. Sponge,
on his return from hunting too late for lunch, that he
had missed a most excellent rabbit pie.

But in the olden time, in the charters of free
warren granted by the Norman and Plantagenet
kings, and before the advent of the pheasant or the
preservation of the partridge, when rangers, fowlers,
and fishermen were always abroad questing in the
woodlands and on the meres, the rabbit received
special attention. Now a warren has come to mean
a space of ground entirely given up to him. Then he
was the smallest, but the most common, of the lesser
beasts of chase. The purveyors of the great barons,
who daily fed in their halls whole troops of hungry
retainers, found him extremely serviceable. More-

over, he was what the cooks of our middle classes call a company dish. At the grand feast given at the installation of the youngest brother of 'the King-maker' as Archbishop of York, in 1467, 4,000 rabbits appear in the bill of fare, taking immediate precedence of as many heronshaws. Archer, in his 'Highways of Letters,' describing ordinary dinners in the time of Chaucer, begins with a pottage, called 'buckernade,' made of fowl or rabbit, cut up fine and stewed, as was the fashion then, with a diabolical variety of spices. The rabbit seems only to have lost caste with the change of dynasty on the demise of Queen Anne ; for the 'rabbit tart' was a standing dish on the table of Her gouty Majesty, who was a noted gourmande and a voracious eater. In 'The Noble Boke of Cookry for a Prynce's Houseolde or any other estately houseolde,' which must have been written about the time of the great Neville banquet, rabbits are always set down in the services for the cooler months. Curiously enough, they seem generally to have been spitted—for, as we have said, a rabbit has no fat, and roasting is the worst use he can be put to. To make him tolerably succulent he must be elabo-rately basted. And no such careful basting could be practicable in the case of cooking four thousand simultaneously. Here are some of those venerable recipes which have historic rather than gastronomic value.

'CONY ROST

'A Conye tak and drawe him and parboile him rost him and lard him then raise his leggs and hys winges and sauce him with vinegar and powder of guinger and serue it.' Or

'RABETTES ROST

'To rost rabettes tak and slay them draw them and rost them and let their heddes be in first parboile them or ye rost them and serue them.'

The sole alternative to the rough and ready 'rost' was the 'cevy,' more artistic and in every way preferable.

'Smyt them in small pieces and sethe them in good brothe put them to mynced onyons and grece and drawe a liour of brown bred and blod and seison it with venygar and cast in pouder and salt and serve it.'

For as apple sauce has always gone with goose, bread sauce with white-fleshed birds, sweet sauce or wine sauce with venison, and barberry sauce with the strong-flavoured Italian wild boar, so onions were from the first associated with the rabbit, and with better reason than some of these other accompaniments. For the flavour of a mild onion is the complement of the modest *goût* of the rabbit, which it brings out by some recondite chemical attraction. The discoverer of the secret deserves well ˙of posterity, though perhaps we are indebted for the sympathetic combination to stress of circumstances ; for when most vegetables were scarce with us, onions were common. Here is a good white onion sauce which, freely translated into French, might be called *à la Soubise.*

Peel a dozen of onions and steep them in salt and water to blanch them. Boil in plenty of water and change it once at least ; chop them and pass them through a sieve, stir them up with melted butter, or roast the onions and pulp them.

For a brown onion sauce, more *prononcé* in flavour. Slice large Spanish onions : brown them in butter over a slow fire, add brown gravy, pepper and salt, and butter rolled in brown flour. Skim and put in a glass of port or Burgundy with half as much ketchup ; or, according to Meg Dodds, whose hints are always invaluable, add a dessert spoonful of walnut pickle or eschalot vinegar with some essence of lemon.

She has a recipe for mushroom sauce for rabbits. ' Wash and pick a large breakfast-cup full of small

button-mushrooms : take off the leathery skin and
stew them in veal gravy, with pepper, cayenne, mace,
nutmeg, salt, and a piece of butter rolled in flour or
arrowroot to thicken, as the abounding gravy of the
mushrooms makes this dish need a good deal of
thickening. Stew till tender, stirring them now and
then, and pour the sauce over the rabbits. Those
who like a high relish of mushroom may add a spoonful of mushroom gravy, or the mushrooms may be
stewed in cream and seasoned and thickened as above.'

It is a good sauce, but, far from needing to
strengthen the mushroom flavour, in our opinion it
is essentially too strong. It somewhat oppresses the
sweet simplicity of the rabbit, whereas, though it
may seem paradoxical, currying appears to elicit it.
This recipe is more suitable ; for celery is the most
harmonious of all concomitants, though it does not
come, like the onion, with a counterblast to provoke
a piquancy :—

Wash, pare and slice the sticks of celery. Blanch
and boil and season with spices and pepper. Flavour
the sauce with an infusion of lemon, but be niggardly
with the condiments, which in excess must neutralise
the flavour of the celery, not to speak of outraging the
susceptibilities of the rabbit.

Allusion to onions and sauces has tempted us on

to the *entrées,* but in the due order of things we must turn back to the soups.   For nothing does the rabbit come in more usefully than for mulligatawny : when that soup is most in request in cool weather, the rabbit is in his best condition; there is as little reason to be frugal with him as with the Ettrick Shepherd's hare soup, and his recipe, if we remember aright, was a half-dozen of hares to the tureen.

Break up sundry rabbits and boil in three quarts of water with a quarter-ounce of black pepper.   Be sure to add a slice or two of bacon.   Skim the stock when it boils, and let it simmer for an hour and a half before straining.   Fry some of the choice morsels of the rabbit with sliced onions in a stewpan; add the strained stock, skim, and, when it has simmered for three-quarters of an hour, throw in two dessert spoonfuls of curry powder, the same quantity of lightly browned flour, with salt and cayenne, and let it simmer again till the meat is thoroughly tender.   A clove or two of garlic, shred and fried in butter, with a dash of lemon to taste, are decided improvements.

N.B. Half the secret and charm of good mulligatawny is in the successful boiling of the rice, which ought to fall light and white and dry, like snowflakes in frost or manna in the wilderness.   The rice after boiling should be drained and dried before the fire in a sieve reversed.

As simple game soup, carve the rabbits carefully and fry with bacon, onions, carrots, &c. Drain and stew for an hour in beef stock, with celery and minced parsley. Small pieces of the rabbits may be fried and stewed in the broth.

As we have seen, there were no rabbits in Meg Merrilies' caldron, but her namesake, Meg Dodds, gives a capital recipe for what she calls Poachers' Soup, or Soupe à la Meg Merrilies, for which rabbits may be used as well as anything else. Meg does not say whether it was the dish invented by M. Florence, *chef* to the Duke of Buccleuch, and served at Bowhill in honour of the author of 'Waverley.'

'This savoury and highly relishing new stew soup may be made of anything or everything known by the name of game. Take from two to four pounds of the trimmings or coarse parts of venison, shin of beef, or shanks or lean scrag of good mutton, all fresh. Break the bones and boil this with a couple of carrots and turnips, four onions, a bunch of parsley and a quarter-ounce of peppercorns. Strain this stock when it has boiled for three hours. Cut down and skin a blackcock, a pheasant, half a hare or a rabbit, &c.,

and season the pieces with mixed spices. These may be floured and browned in the frying-pan, but as this is a process dictated by the eye as much as the palate, it is not necessary in this soup. Put the game to the strained stock with a dozen of small onions, a couple of heads of celery sliced, half a dozen peeled potatoes, and, when it boils, a small white cabbage quartered, black pepper, allspice and salt to taste. Let the soup simmer till the game is tender but not overdone.' The soup may be coloured and flavoured with red wine and a couple of spoonfuls of mushroom ketchup.

It is an admirable dish for the gypsies of Dern-cleugh or the phenomenal gourmands of the *Noctes Ambrosianæ*, but obviously far too solid for the foundation of a refined banquet. So we suspect that M. Florence's rendering was a more sublimated version of the original, although he catered for salmon-fishers, shooters and coursers.

We have said that roasting is the worst use to which you can put a rabbit, and we repeat it. But if you will roast, see that the rabbit is well basted. Skin and draw, leaving the ears ; dip them in boiling water and scrape off the hairs ; pick out the eyes ; cut off the feet ; wash in cold water and dry with a cloth, and cut the sinews at the back of the hind

R

quarters and below the fore-legs. Prepare some savoury stuffing and fill the inside; then draw the legs under, set the head between the shoulders and stick a skewer through them, passing through the neck; run another skewer through the fore-legs, to be gathered up under the haunches; take string, double it, place the middle in the breast, and carry both ends over the skewer; cross the string on both sides, and fasten it. Spit and roast for an hour before a brisk fire, constantly basting with fresh dripping. Five minutes before serving dredge with flour and baste with fresh butter. When the rabbit has been richly browned, remove the string and skewers, dish it, and serve with brown gravy.

For boiling, rabbits should be trussed neatly and boiled slowly. It is far better to overdo than to underdo, and they will take a full hour, unless very young and tender. They will be none the worse for an addition in the boiling of some suet and slices of lemon. To fry them, they are first cut up and done slowly in butter with sage and dried parsley. The liver may be crushed in a parsley sauce, and the parsley which the rabbit loved in life should be fried and strewed around him when he is sent to table. A variation is rabbit *aux fines herbes*.

'Carve two plump young rabbits, and fry the

pieces in butter with grated bacon and a handful of chopped mushrooms, parsley and eschalot, with salt and pepper. Boil a teaspoonful of flour with a little *consommé*, and pour into the stew-pan with the rabbits. Stew slowly; skin and strain the sauce and serve it on the rabbits with lemon and cayenne.' A faint suspicion of garlic improves all these dishes. There is no better way of disposing of rabbits than smothering. Truss and boil and smother in creamy onion sauce. Mrs. Dodds tells us that in Scotland they used to be smothered in an onion sauce made with clear gravy instead of melted butter, and that, if the dish looked less attractive, it was equally good. Whether rabbits are boiled to be smothered or boiled to be served *au naturel*, the essential is that the boiling should be as slow as possible and finished leisurely in front of the fire.

Rabbit curry is always capital, and, if economy is to be considered, the fragments of former dishes may be utilised. The great thing is to make sure of good stock, and the cook's skill is shown in suiting the seasoning to the palates of those who are to partake. Tastes vary; but it is obvious enough that the savour of the rabbit should not be swamped in too fiery a dressing. The cut meat is fried in butter with sliced Portugal onions over a quick fire. The artist must of course pay attention to the colouring, which ought to be soft Vandyke brown or glowing amber. When the colouring is achieved, add a pint of the stock, let it simmer for a quarter of an hour, throw in the curry powder with a spoonful of flour, and stir them into the sauce. When the curry is ready add another glass of cream, with a strong squeeze of the lemon. A clove of mild garlic will not be out of place, and for Indians who prefer a curry strongly spiced add a few capsicums or a lively chili.

Mr. Jawleyford was not far wrong in his praise of a good pie, but much of the excellence depends on a judicious use of adjuncts. Mushrooms are almost indispensable, and even the freshest truffles are not wasted. Slices of egg are a decided improvement, and some people advocate forcemeat balls, though that is more open to question. At any rate, there can be no doubt about eschalots, anchovies, or Norwegian sprats, with butter or shred suet. But, above all, the pie should be paved with slices of fat bacon, and bacon should be interpolated through the pieces of rabbit. Strain the gravy, which should be boiled to a jelly. Crown with a rich puff-paste, and bake the pie according to size. Patties follow pie in natural sequence, and they make a convenient *entrée* for the economical housekeeper. Mince the best

parts of cold rabbits with some fine-shred suet. Get
some good gravy, thicken with butter and flour, and
season to taste with the inevitable lemon juice. Add
a little claret or port—though the strictly economical
may dispense with that—and a dash of chili or
tarragon vinegar. Stew the mince and fill the patties,
which had best be baked empty.

Boudins de Richelieu probably owe their name
to the *roué* lover of the Duchesse de Berri, one of
the volatile daughters of the Regent Orleans. Richelieu was as great, though scarcely so scientific, a
gourmet as the Regent, who was as much at home in
his kitchens as in his chemical laboratory ; and the
lady, by the way, is said to have prided herself on
having devised the delicate *filets de lapereau*. The
boudins are made of a forcemeat of rabbit beaten up
with grated potatoes. Dressed onions or chopped
mushrooms must be mixed with the stuffing. The
forcemeat is rolled up in small sausages, then it is
boiled or baked and served with brown sauce. It is
the more probable that Richelieu invented these
boudins, that the dish survives in the French *haute
cuisine*, and is the only form of the rabbit in cookery
which Dubois condescends to notice in his portly
volume de luxe. Possibly Dubois may have descended
from the disreputable Abbé and Cardinal who was

the Regent's *âme damné*. Dubois gives the recipe with a *purée* of chestnuts, and prefaces it thus : 'This is a forcemeat *entrée*, pleasant, good, and offering great resources when the shooting season is over. With care it can be rendered *distingué* and elegant.

'Forcemeat made of young rabbits must be prepared in the same proportions as that of the pheasant ; it must be worked for a few minutes with a spoon and a little melted glaze introduced, with a few table-spoonfuls of pickled tongue cut in the shape of very small dice. It is divided in pieces of the size of an egg, which are to fall on the floured table and be rolled with the hand so as to give them an oval form of the size of a cutlet.' N.B.—Mrs. Dodds gives the counsel of perfection, that the *boudins* should be rolled with a knife.

'These *boudins* are ranged in a *sautoir*, so as to poach them in boiling, salted water ; as soon as they are become firm, they are drained and trimmed in an oval form and bread-crumbed. Some clarified butter is warmed in a *sautoir*, the *boudins* ranged on its surface and coloured on a sharp fire, turning them at the same time. When fried to a nice colour, they are drained and dished in a circular order round a pyramid of chestnut *purée*. A sauceboat of reduced espagnole is served at the same time.'

For cream of rabbit, the meat is pounded to a pulp in a mortar, passed through a sieve, then worked up with the yolks of several eggs, a gill of rich cream, seasoned with pepper, salt and nutmeg. When the blend is perfectly smooth, butter a mould, arrange thin slices of truffles at the bottom ; then put in the mixture, which should barely fill half the mould ; tie paper on the top ; place the mould in boiling water and steam it for an hour and a half. Serve with truffle sauce, or, failing truffles, with tomatoes.

For Rabbit mould, make a case of paste in a mould of flour and water ; line the mould with it, fill up with dry flour and put it in the oven to brown ; leave it in the shape till cold, then turn it out. Remove the dry flour and egg the outside. Cut up a young rabbit or two ; stew in gravy with a little onion and a few cloves till the gravy is thick ; when ready heat the case in the oven ; turn the stew into the shape, and dish on a napkin.

For Cutlets.—Cut out the fillets from the backs of two rabbits ; cut each in halves and shape as cutlets, season with salt and pepper. Stick a morsel of rib into the end of each ; egg and bread-crumb them ; fry them to a bright brown and serve with sauce to taste. Slices of bacon or ham should be sandwiched between the pieces of rabbit, and asparagus tops, mushrooms, or other vegetables may be served in the centre.

Mrs. Henry Reeve, in her judicious work on Cookery, gives an American recipe for barbecuing :—

'Clean and wash the rabbit, which must be plump and young, and having opened it all the way on the under side, lay it flat, with a small plate to keep it down in salted water for half an hour. Wipe dry and broil whole, with the exception of the head, when you have gashed across the backbone in eight or ten places, that the heat may penetrate this, the thickest part. The fire should be hot and clear, the rabbit turned often. When browned and tender, lay upon a very hot dish, pepper and salt and butter profusely, turning the rabbit over and over to soak up the melted butter. Cover, and set in the oven for five minutes, and heat in a tin cup two tablespoonfuls of vinegar seasoned with one of made mustard. Anoint the hot rabbit well with this, cover and send to table garnished with crisp parsley.'

Finally, the head is not to be neglected. It contains a variety of delicate picking, and gives light, desultory occupation to a wayward appetite.

INDEX

Spottiswoode & Co. Printers, New-street Square, London